NESHANI ANDREAS was ~~born~~
1964. She trained as a teach~~er~~
College. This is her first nove~~l~~.

NESHANI ANDREAS

THE PURPLE VIOLET OF OSHAANTU

Heinemann

Heinemann Educational Publishers
Halley Court, Jordan Hill, Oxford OX2 8EJ
A Division of Reed Educational & Professional Publishing Ltd

Heinemann: A Division of Reed Publishing (USA) Inc.
361 Hanover Street, Portsmouth, NH 03801–3912, USA

Heinemann Publishers (Pty) Limited
PO Box 781940, Sandton 2146, Johannesburgh, South Africa

OXFORD   MELBOURNE   AUCKLAND
JOHANNESBURG   BLANTYRE   GABORONE
IBADAN   PORTSMOUTH (NH) USA   CHICAGO

Available in Zimbabwe from Weaver Press

© Neshani Andreas 2001

First published by Heinemann Educational Publishers in 2001

British Library Cataloguing in Publication Data
A catalogue record for this book is available from the British Library.

Cover design by Amanda Carroll
Cover illustration by Steve Rawlings

Phototypeset by SetSystems Ltd, Saffron Walden, Essex
Printed and bound in Great Britain by
Cox and Wyman Ltd, Reading, Berkshire

ISBN 0 435 91208 9

01 02 03 04 05 06 07 08 8 7 6 5 4 3 2 1

Dedication

To my dear father, Tate Andreas Nkoshi, for your incredible strengths, with loving memories. May your soul rest in His everlasting peace.

and

To my mother, Gwambetu Mushelenga, for your dignity.

With gratitude to:

Namupongo (He who created Himself) for Your unconditional love; Mrs Jane Katjavivi, for closing your door to open mine – I am forever grateful to you; the Heinemann family, for helping me realise my childhood dream; Risto Kapenda, for your uncensored constructive criticism, but most importantly for believing in me; Lishan Wodageneh, my sister and angel, for your love; Brett 'Mboloto' Jebens, for your support across the Atlantic; Randy Shigwele, my 'godson', your support has been humbling; Tate Shiimi–ya–Shiimi, for your generous advice; Pastor Petrus Kim and Petrus Haakskeen for being my role models; my brothers and sisters, Garincha, Sacky, Selma, Nanona, Johny, Hilma and Hilmatjie, for your support; Peace Corps Volunteers Reed Dickson, Agai Jones, Lilly Asrat, Sue Tellingator and Karla Wynn, for supporting my work; my teachers at Immanuel Ruiters Primary School, Walvis Bay, Ongwediva Teachers College and the University of Namibia; and my Mbushe, Neshani M. Biegen, for the sunshine that you are. I love you all!

Chapter One

It is that time of the year again. The season when our village, Oshaantu, camouflages itself in a rich green carpet and provides a breathtaking sight, especially from our homestead, which is built on an incline. I wish time would stand still. We had good rains this year and are promised plenty to eat. My heart is full of gratitude as I look at all the *omahangu*, sorghum, spinach, beans, pumpkins, watermelons, nuts, corn and cabbage. Those of us who worked the extra mile will not have to buy tomatoes, onions, sweet potatoes and guavas for a good while. I gently stroke the rough surface of the *omahangu* millet in appreciation of the abundance of Mother Nature. God is good, I think.

'Oh, halloo Mee Maita, I didn't see you coming,' I say apologetically.

'I thought as much,' Mee Maita replies with a smile.

'I was looking at all this,' I say, both my hands pointing towards the green sward that lies before us.

'We will have a good harvest this year. I don't remember having so much rain since I was a child,' Meme Maita observes, looking up at the sky as if for more rain. '*Omwa lala po ngaa, Mee Ali,*'* she then greets me formally.

'*Eee, ne mwa lala po wo, Mee Maita,*'† I respond to her greetings.

She asks about my mother-in-law and my children.

---

* 'Did you sleep well, Mee Ali?'
† 'I slept well, if you slept well, Mee Maita.'

'They are fine,' I say, looking at the homestead from where their voices can be heard. Then I ask about her family.

'They are all fine as well,' she replies, nodding. 'And how is Tate Michael? Have you heard anything from him lately?' she enquires about my husband.

'Yes, we received a letter from him last month. It came with one of the Kapendas' sons.'

'I trust he is doing well?'

'Oh yes, he's doing fine. He told us that if his employers will allow him, he will come home during the long Easter weekend, otherwise I will visit him in May.' I rub the back of my neck, avoiding her eyes. I don't mention all the goodies that Michael sent us, as I only gave a small portion of them to my best friend, Meme Kauna. Life is expensive nowadays and one cannot afford to share things around as we once used to.

'Please, pass my family's kind regards to your husband next time you write to him,' she says.

'Thank you, Mee Maita. I will definitely do so.'

'Well, I just stopped by to greet you. I am on my way to church to prepare for Sunday school tomorrow and put clean tablecloths on the altar for the church service,' she continues, looking at the contents of her basket.

'Well, thank you, Mee Maita, it is always good to see you,' I respond, knowing this is not wholly true.

She looks at me. I rub the back of my neck again.

'*Shilwii po nawa ano, Mee Ali*,'* she bids me goodbye.

'*Eewa, nane ka shilwii po nawa, Mee Maita*.'†

Mee Maita is about to leave when the sound of a car makes us turn our heads. I immediately recognise the green Chevrolet that belongs to our neighbour, Tate Shange, as he drives it down the gravel road that separates our homestead from theirs.

* 'Have a pleasant morning, Mee Ali.'
† 'Thank you, and you have a nice morning too, Mee Maita.'

He parks the car under a huge *marula* tree on their *omahangu* field, steps out of the vehicle, slams the door and disappears into his homestead.

I should be used to this by now, I think, but I feel angry every time I see Shange behaving like this towards his wife. His latest extra-marital affair is with a young woman from the nearby village. He is often seen with her at the *cuca* shop belonging to his friend, the local teacher, Mr Jackson. Shange has built her a two-roomed blockhouse, painted white. Since then his wife Kauna and I have nicknamed her the woman from the 'white house'. Shange does not even bother to conceal his relationship. His car is often seen in broad daylight parked in front of the white house. I turn to Meme Maita, who is still staring at Shange's Chevrolet.

'Meme Maita, look where the sun is! Is this really the way a Christian should behave? Why does he have to come at this time? I don't think he has any respect for his wife at all! To do this so publicly!'

'Maybe he has an emergency,' she replies.

'Meme Maita, we all know he has a . . .'

'Yes, we all know he has this woman. All I am saying is that maybe he is coming from somewhere else, from a sick relative or so,' she interrupts me.

I look at her, scrutinising her face. Why does she always tie her bandanna so close to her eyes? She looks so ugly, I think, feeling suddenly irritated at the very sight of her.

'Well, dear, let me leave you now. I have to finish the church preparations before the sun sits here,' she says, pointing to a position in the sky indicating the midday hour.

This woman will never change, I think. My morning is ruined!

◆

Meme Maita is one of those people about whom I can never make up my mind. She is just too confusing for me to understand. Sometimes I think she tries too hard to be a Christian, and sometimes I think she just needs a good friend. But one thing I'm sure of is that she pretends to like me though I know she doesn't. Actually, the antipathy is mutual. However, she is a respected and somehow powerful member of the village because she is an elder in the church and a Sunday school teacher. So she is one of those who decides who will be forgiven and who will not be. What I most dislike about her is that she does either little or nothing for the women and widows who are mistreated by their husbands and in-laws, despite her position. She believes that marriage should be one miserable, lifelong experience. Husband and wife should fight every day, he should abuse her and the children, he should go after other women, otherwise '*okwa tulwa mo*'.* It is the way of the world. She never has anything good to say about marriage.

'This is what marriage is all about. This is the real world. You have promised to stay in this thing till death do you part,' are her usual responses to marriage problems. I often argue with her.

'No, Mee Maita, marriage doesn't need to be a miserable thing. I am not saying there will be no problems, but you always make it sound as if marriage was a funeral.'

'This is just because you are a new bride. It was like that for all of us in the beginning, it was wonderful. I am not exaggerating or trying to scare you, but the truth is marriage is very, very difficult. One day you will say, "Mee Maita, you told me so".'

You can't win an argument with this woman, I think, feeling

---

* Literally, 'he is stuffed in her anus': the equivalent would be 'he is under her thumb'.

discouraged. I have been married for eleven years now and I haven't wanted to cry on her shoulder once.

Why are people suspicious about a loving husband? What is strange about a good father? What is evil about a man who does not abuse his woman and children? These are questions I have asked Kauna and myself on numerous occasions; usually we don't find answers.

◆

About three years ago, I sent a message to Mee Maita with the kind-hearted and highly respected Tate Mbenjameni, one of the church elders. I told him that I had a problem and I wanted to talk to a sister, preferably Mee Maita. Like a faithful man of God, he went to see her and returned with a response.

'She said you could see her this week, Saturday,' Tate Mbenjameni informed me.

'This Saturday already?'

'Yes, this Saturday, around this time,' he said, pointing to the sky and indicating the morning at around ten o'clock. He looked at me, his eyes full of pity.

'It is always good to talk, you know. It is not good to keep things in here,' he said, putting his right hand on his chest. 'Mee Maita is a woman of God and you can trust her with anything. Rest assured that whatever you discuss with her will remain between the two of you,' he continued confidently.

'Thank you very much, Tate Mbenjameni, I really appreciate your efforts.'

'It is nothing child, it is really nothing. I am just glad to help,' he assured me, his bald head shining in the sun. He is always officially dressed in a suit and tie, even in this heat. Sunday to Sunday. Does he ever work in the fields? My eyes followed his short, slender body as he left. I was happy he did not ask why I wanted to see Mee Maita. Tate Mbenjameni only sees good in people. His trust in them is almost childlike. So you have to form your own judgements. He is too trusting.

On Saturday morning I prepared myself to go to Mee Maita. She was unusually happy to see me. Their homestead was spacious, with many mud huts. Purple and white violets grew beside the fence. She led me through the house to a large private hut where she obviously receives her guests. The room was clean and neat. On the mud floor was a beautiful black and white mat made from the skin of a once very big cow. She invited me to sit on the mat and joined me soon afterwards.

I was surprised by her hospitality and the obvious efforts she had made to receive me. There was food and drinks. I realised that she had also brewed some *omalovu* for me. That surprised me still more, as we all know that preparing *omalovu* takes a long time – a day and a half or so. I never knew she held me in such high esteem! She reached for the calabash full of *omalovu* and pulled it closer to her, took an *ompamba* and used it to pour some of the liquid into two, beautifully crafted *iitenga*. She took a sip from my *omalovu* before she gave it to me, a sign that she had no ill feelings.

'Thank you,' I whispered, and took a sip. I felt bad about all the negative things I had ever said and thought about her. All the judgements I had passed on her. God forgive me, I thought.

'This is the best *omalovu* I have tasted in a very long time,' I said. She smiled. I emptied my *oshitenga*. She filled it again, full. I didn't drink it immediately. I put it on the floor beside me. I thought I should wait for her.

She drank her *oshitenga* half way and started to make preparations for us to eat. She removed the *elilo* that covered the two *omatemba* and clay pots. She had prepared *oshithima*, the main dish, and a variety of dishes to go with it: beef, chicken, *evanda* and dried caterpillars. The smell of food immediately filled the hut. She brought another small black clay pot with *ondjove* oil. Mmm! How I love the smell of *ondjove*, not to mention eating it with *evanda* and *oshithima*. My mouth watered. I reached for my *oshitenga* and emptied it. I thought I should probably start talking while she was dishing out the food.

'Well, Mee Maita, as Tate Mbenjameni told you, I need to talk to you, about a personal matter.'

'Yes, my sister. Tate Mbenjameni said so, and as I told him, the sooner the better. Come, let's talk. I will listen to your problems,' she answered quite eagerly; too eagerly, I thought. She continued to dish out the food. It looked good.

'Mee Maita, I choose to come to you because you have been a church elder for many years. The other sisters are fairly new and might not have dealt with this kind of problem before. Besides, Tate Mbenjameni said I could trust you and advised me not to keep things inside,' I told her.

'Thank you,' she said, her expression revealing that she felt quite flattered. 'I agree with Tate Mbenjameni, it is not good to keep things in the heart. You know, Mee Ali, I always tell the women at the choir and at the Wednesday evening meetings that my doors are wide open for any one of them to come and discuss their problems with me. Sometimes I can tell that some of the women have problems just by looking at them. Especially when they have those mysterious bruises or start to lose weight. But they don't come to me. When I ask out of concern, they feel offended or they say they have no problems, but I . . .'

'Mee Maita,' I interrupted her.

'Yes, my sister,' she said and gave me a smile I did not trust.

'My husband doesn't know that I have come to see you,' I went on with a warning smile.

'My sister,' she put her right hand on my shoulder while giving me her 'sympathetic' stare, 'this is between you and me.'

She gave my shoulder a slight squeeze: 'that is, unless you want me to mention it to the church elders.'

'Of course not!'

'Then I will not say a word,' she assured me and again she sounded too eager to hear what I was going to tell her. She took my *oshitenga* and filled it again.

I took a long sip before I started to talk. Mee Maita was terribly disappointed when I informed her that I had come to talk about Kauna's marriage problems. Her face dropped. She was clearly taken aback by the turn of events and could hardly conceal her disappointment. I realised that she was curious about me. She thought I was going to talk about myself. What did she think I would tell her? 'Remember, Mee Maita, you told me? Now I know. You were right. Men are dogs!' Nevertheless I went ahead and explained the purpose of my visit. I told her how I felt about Kauna's marriage, although I knew she was already well aware of her problems.

'Mee Maita, I am really not happy with the way Shange treats his wife. He mistreats her time and time again. The other day he almost killed her when he beat her. The whole village knew about it.'

'Ya,' she said, as if she were bored.

'I was thinking, maybe you could talk to the elders. Maybe the church could find a permanent solution to their marriage problems,' I said, trusting that I had used the right words.

Feebly she promised to look into the matter. It was obvious that she was not interested in talking about Kauna's marriage.

We ate in silence. She was a good cook. Occasionally I would look at her. She didn't look at me. At one point I thought the food would choke her – she looked as if she had difficulty swallowing it. Ha, she probably thought she was going to hear *it all*!

Despite the fact that my visit to Mee Maita and our discussion were supposed to be 'confidential', the whole village heard about them. I did not think I would survive that rumour. The men hated me. They thought I was a bad influence. The women thought I was self-righteous. Shange ignored me whenever he could. My husband gave me a lecture!

'Ali, I think this time you went too far. For you to ask the church to end Shange and Kauna's marriage. Are you crazy? You are not God. You will not solve the problems of all the women in this village. It looks as though you want to jump in and fix everything, every time Kauna confides in you. Maybe she doesn't even expect you to sort out her problems. Maybe she only wants you to lend her your ear. Have you ever thought of this?

'And now the men are looking at me badly. They talk behind my back, they say that I have a wife who is not disciplined. Please, I don't want to go through this again. The only reason why Shange did not come here to give you a piece of his mind is because I have named our daughter after his wife.'

Michael went on without giving me a chance to tell my side of the story. 'Now promise that you will not interfere in the Shanges' problems again and that you will never ever try to fix them. Do you hear me!'

My husband had never talked to me like that before. I cried. He lowered his voice.

'Look, I have always admired the way you care about people and I love this about you.'

I cried harder.

'But please, understand, you need to stay away from other people's marriage problems. Do you understand?'

I nodded.

'So you promise?'

Like a little girl, I promised not to interfere with Kauna and Shange's marriage problems. I was furious and embarrassed at the same time. I wanted to go and confront the old cow. I did not talk to Mee Maita for months.

◆

I had been less than half an hour in my hut when I heard the screams. For a moment I was confused, trying to figure out who was screaming and where the sound was coming from.

'It is from Tate Shange's homestead,' my children shouted.

I recognised my friend Kauna's voice immediately. I ran to their homestead as fast as I could. I arrived to find everything upside down. The children were crying and Kauna was hysterical. She stood beside the fresh marks left by her husband's car. She was screaming and shouting, her arms flying everywhere about her.

'He just came home, he just came home. Ask my children. Ask my children. Ask them. He just came home,' she said over and over again. She pointed at the fresh tyre treads. 'See, he didn't sleep here last night, he just came home this morning. See, see the lines, he came a few moments ago.'

Nothing made any sense to me. The children crying, and my friend in a strange mood. I was confused.

'Kauna, what is going on? What is happening? Please tell me!' I pleaded with her.

'It is . . . it is . . . Dad . . . Daddy,' Kauna's eleven-year-old daughter Kandiwapa told me, tears pouring from her eyes.

'What about Daddy?' I asked, but without waiting for an answer I went to look for Shange myself. I went to their concrete-roomed house. The door to the living room was wide open. I was quite unprepared for what I saw. I did not expect the man I had seen only a few minutes ago to be dead. My body went cold. I didn't know what to do – whether to scream or run away. I stood there like a statue. I couldn't move. My legs felt as if they would give way under me at any moment. Dead? No! It can't be so, I thought.

'I think he is dead,' somebody said behind my back.

I quickly turned around. It was Tate Arumasa, one of our neighbours. I became aware of people in the room and their curious looks.

Kauna, where is she? Where is Kauna? I thought out loud. I hurried out of the room, squeezing through the crowd that was gathering. I almost bumped into her. She was leading a group of about five people into the living room.

'Come and see for yourself, his food is still there,' she waved at them.

Shange was in a sitting position, his head had flopped forward like somebody who was sleeping in his chair. Kauna almost tripped over his body as she hurried to show them his food. She ignored Shange completely. She lifted the lid covering the food that was evidently the supper he had not eaten last night.

'See? He did not touch any of the food I prepared for him,' she said, holding the lid away with both her hands. 'He did not eat my food. Ask my children,' she kept repeating. The dazed look in her eyes seemed to indicate that she was a million kilometres away. It was as if she did not know or recognise me. She did not cry. There were no tears on her face, not one.

'Ask my children, please people, ask my children. He did not eat my food,' she kept repeating. She put the lid down without covering the food. Suddenly she looked at me. 'Do you believe me?' she asked. I opened my mouth only to close it again.

Without waiting for an answer she hurried out of the living room. I followed her outside. We saw Kandiwapa, and Kauna grabbed her arm. 'Tell them! Did Daddy eat his food?' Kandiwapa cried more from shock at the way in which her mother was behaving, than from the strength of her grasp.

11

Then, without warning, Kauna dropped her daughter's arm and marched over to where her husband's car was parked. Barefoot, her hair uncombed, wearing an outsize dress that hung loosely over her body exposing one shoulder and half of her breast, she marched to and fro between the living room and the fresh lines that the car had left in the soil. Kauna was behaving like some of the mentally disturbed women we have in our village. I felt sure she had lost her mind.

'Stop there! Don't walk there!' she yelled at people who had started to examine the tyre treads on the road. Kauna shocked almost everybody who arrived. She was not behaving like a widow. She walked straight up to the villagers and told them that her husband had not slept at home last night and had not eaten her food this morning.

I tried to stop her without causing a scene. But she hurried to the living room once more as if she sensed my intention to stop her. I followed her. I noticed that they had removed Shange's body. She acted as if she did not notice. She pulled up a chair and sat down. She began chanting rhythmically as if she had no plans to leave the living room.

'Kauna, you cannot go on like this. Stop talking about the food you prepared and go to your room,' I said to her. All of a sudden she started to yell.

'People must know the truth. He did not eat my food and I did not kill him! You hear me. You hear me. You evil people. I know what you are thinking. I know because you are evil. Evil people, all of you!' She was screaming, pointing at all of us in the living room.

'Of course you did not kill him. What are you talking about? How can you even think that? Nobody thinks you killed your husband . . .'

She looked at me as if I had said the funniest thing on earth and laughed hysterically.

'Listen, Kauna, your husband is dead. Shange is dead and you must accept it. You are a widow now. Come let's go to your room. What will people think of your behaviour?' I was trying not to sound harsh or judgemental. I gently pulled her off the sofa, towards the bedroom she had shared with Shange for so many years.

'Don't let them take away his food,' she pleaded, looking back at the food. 'Please don't let them. Stop them, please stop them, please . . .' she pleaded, her voice becoming smaller and smaller.

'Nobody will take away his food. Nobody will,' I assured her. I escorted her to their bedroom as if she were an unwilling little girl. At the door she froze.

'Kauna . . .' I said, becoming a little impatient.

'I don't want to go in there, I don't want to.'

'Okay, okay, Kauna, where do you want to go?'

'To my hut.' She looked away as if to avoid protest from me. I escorted her to her hut.

'What has got into her? Is she sick?' people asked curiously. Soon everybody had heard what had happened. That her husband did not sleep at home – just arrived in the morning – did not eat her food, and had died. But the biggest news in the village was that Kauna had gone mad.

More neighbours, friends and relatives arrived and soon the house was overflowing. Shange's relatives were especially helpful in making sure that everybody was taken care of. Women soon found something to do; they busied themselves with cooking and feeding people and taking care of Shange's children.

◆

After a long struggle to keep Kauna in her hut she fell asleep – exhausted. Her hut was the place where she sometimes received

13

close friends, but mostly she used it when she wanted to be alone. It was obvious that she had not been in it for some time. Her clothes and other personal belongings lay all over the place, some on the bed and others on the floor. Three of her church dresses hung on wire hangers hooked to the thatched roof. An Afro comb and a pair of crochet pins were also stuck into the thatch.

If Kauna wanted to be in this room, then people would be coming into it to express their sympathy and condolences, I thought. So, I decided to tidy up a bit. I folded all her clothes neatly and packed them in a half-open suitcase under her bed. I pulled the church dresses together, against the mud wall, to create more space to move in the room. The small items, a container of Vaseline, a bar of soap and a roll-on deodorant, I packed neatly in a big box, which she used as a dressing table. There was a tree trunk that served as a chair. I pushed it against the wall opposite the bed. I lifted the mat and shook it a couple of times. I took a straw broom and swept all the dry grass and leaves from the hut.

The sweeping threw up a lot of dust. Kauna, who was still sleeping, started to cough uncontrollably. I stopped sweeping and watched her, hoping that if I remained still, she would not wake up. She had thrown her body right across the three-quarter bed like a person who was drunk. She moved once more and turned to face the mud wall. I continued to clean, moving about very quietly. At last the room was presentable enough to receive guests.

One thing about death is that it comes so unexpectedly that it finds you totally unprepared; at times, with an untidy house and no money or support from relatives and friends – just as when poor old Namene died. Kuku Namene and her husband lived with their grandchildren. There were no other adults around. The old couple depended on the charity and goodwill of their neighbours and young people from the village, who often went to their homestead to pound for them or assisted them by fetching water and wood or with other household chores. Their homestead was poorly built. The sticks of the fence were old and collapsing. Not a single decent mud hut existed in their compound. Mourners had nowhere to sit or sleep. There was not enough food to eat or mugs to drink from. Worst of all, not a single animal was slaughtered in honour of the poor woman. The children were accused of neglecting their parents. Their eldest son didn't even come home to help bury his mother. Despite efforts by the neighbours to trace him on national radio, he was nowhere to be found. Rumour had it that he was in Karasburg, or was it Karibib? His other children were living in town, mainly in Windhoek, and would rarely come home except to dump their babies on their parents. They would then disappear until the next pregnancy. 'How someone can leave a baby in the care of people who need care themselves is beyond my understanding,' one mourner complained. Mourners cursed the children because they claimed that they had killed their mother. People talked about old Namene's funeral for a long time. Kauna is fortunate – the Shanges are wealthy people. They own many cattle and large pieces of land.

A little after midday, Shange's cousin Meme Sofia brought lunch for Kauna and me. Kauna was still sleeping and I was not sure if I should wake her up. I ate a little. As her friend, neighbour and 'mother', I was expected to be with her to give her emotional support.

◆

Kauna had been my neighbour and friend since I arrived in Oshaantu eleven years ago. She was one of the few people who was genuinely kind to me and who had welcomed me and

15

taken me in. She had been married for about four years when I arrived in the village. The two of us immediately connected. We became inseparable. My husband, sensing the bond of friendship between us, named our only daughter after Kauna. It was a pleasant surprise. I was delighted by his gesture. I had no words to thank him. I started to call Kauna 'omumwandje' and she would call me 'meme'. My mother-in-law was of course furious that her son's first daughter was not named after her. She did not talk to me for some time. I was called names again: 'I have got him right under my thumb,' I have done this and that to her son to make him love me more. I had been hoping to have another girl, just so that my husband could name her after my mother-in-law and I could find peace of mind. But instead we had six boys and then we gave up. Well, these are things I have no control over. It is God who gives us children and He decides about their sexes.

I had hoped that Michael would ask me to marry him then, before my stomach grew too large, but he said there was no hurry, we should wait until our baby was born and then we would get married. I thought this was just an excuse to get rid of me. He was probably going to marry somebody else, a nurse or a teacher. 'Men . . . !' I thought at the time. But then he never deserted me, not for a moment. However, I learned after our marriage from some of his relatives, the ones who 'liked' me, of the things that were said when Michael informed his family that he intended to marry me.

'Why are you doing this to me, to us, to your family?' his mother challenged him, apparently hurt. 'Why do you want her? Her of all people? Her with those hands that look like chicken claws. That one with the high hips and small legs that make her look like a wild cow. Why, why my son? There are so many good girls around here, decent girls who will make you happier than that woman ever will.'

When it became clear to his mother that he was adamant and would marry me, she changed tactics. She decided to degrade me.

'Why do you want to marry an *oshikumbu*?'

'Mother, please, please,' he said. 'Ali is not a whore. She is the mother of my son and I will not let you talk about her like that.'

'A woman who opens her legs so easily for any man is not a woman, she is a whore. And besides, how do you know it is *your* son?' his mother yelled.

'I am sorry if you don't like her. I love her and she is the woman I am going to marry,' he said with finality and left.

'In the good old days the headman would have burnt you two alive!' his mother yelled after him.

'I knew it. I knew it,' my mother-in-law continued long after Michael had left them. 'The day I saw Ali's mother dragging her daughter to our house, to confront my son with her so-called pregnancy, I knew they were low born. People with no class. Instead of sending a delegation, that woman came herself, and unannounced!'

'And presented herself so poorly,' my sister-in-law Sana said, supporting her mother.

'My son is headed for trouble and he does not see it. But just wait . . .'

'Whores always get good men. I swear she has given my brother some mountain *mutakati*. He is abnormally in love!' Mother and sister-in-law gossiped about me.

'Oh yes, our uncle is completely under petticoat government,' another relative added.

I was so angry when I heard all this that I wanted to go and confront *everybody*, mother-in-law or no mother-in-law, and his fat-ass, lazy sister, Sana. My husband was literally on his knees. He begged me not to confront his relatives. When I

17

cooled off, I was happy I had not done so. How can I confront my mother-in-law with such rumours? It would be disrespectful. However, Michael warned them all. Even those who 'liked' me. He told them to stay away from me and not to offer me any more rumours. You should have seen my husband – his behaviour reminded me of the way my brothers used to protect me at school against the bullies, so that later I could stick out my tongue to them.

◆

On the other hand, naming our daughter after Shange's wife served me and Kauna well. Shange respected me more than ever before. I became his 'mother-in-law' and he my 'son-in-law'. '*Shitenya*' and '*Mememweno*' was what we would affectionately call each other, especially when he was in a good mood. I became Kauna's 'mother' and she my 'daughter'. I exploited this situation whenever I needed favours from Shange. Referring to my daughter, I would say to Shange,

'Your wife is growing fast.'

'Your wife has prepared this for you.'

'Greetings from your wife.'

'Your wife has done this or that.'

And when he was not nice to his wife, I would use the same tactics. 'Please don't treat my daughter like that.'

Even Kauna took advantage of this situation. She would use affectionate remarks about him to my daughter, 'Go say "hi" to our husband.'

Shange was a complete bundle of contradictions. He was nice to some people, arrogant to others and usually mean to his wife. However, he had never been rude to me or my husband as he was sometimes known to be in the village. He would rarely refuse when I asked if Kauna could accompany me to various functions or when I asked for favours on her behalf. For that, I was extremely grateful. Whenever Shange went to the 'white house', or on any of his 'visits', then it was usually time for Kauna and me to go and 'fetch water or wood'. We picked the site or pit furthest away. On those walks we came to know each other better and better.

'After your wedding, how long did your husband take before he built you your kitchen?' I asked Kauna one day when we went to 'fetch water'.

'About a year or so.'

'A year?'

'Yes, more or less.'

'And to build your homestead?'

'A year and a half.'

'Kauna. You shared your in-laws' kitchen for an entire year and lived in their homestead for two and a half years. Two and a half years! But you talk like someone who stayed with them for a weekend. I couldn't possibly have stayed *that* long with *those* people. They would have absolutely suffocated me!'

'Ali, two and a half years is not too long, when you consider women who have lived with their in-laws for more than ten years before their husbands built their homesteads. Others have lived with their in-laws all their lives. I tell you, I know of such people. Don't you?'

'I do, I also know of such women. I guess I forget these things sometimes. But I would certainly die before my time if I had to share a homestead with my in-laws for the rest of my precious life.'

'No, you would not die, you would leave and live.'

'Come on, I'm not that impatient. But tell me, how did you spend all those years with those people?'

'My small mother, Meme Fennie, prepared me for many of the things I encountered at my in-laws'. She is a talkative

19

woman, but talks sense, she is not just a *nyee nyee nyee* type of a person. I really want you to meet her. Then you will know what I'm talking about. She is the only person who seems to understand how I feel about my marriage.

'The first days were difficult. I cried every night. I felt lonely and homesick. I didn't know a soul in the village. I would look for every chance to get away from my in-laws. I would go to fetch water, wood or whatever, just to be able to cry in private.' She looked at me. 'I think you should marry within your own village, in your own surroundings, to somebody you know.'

I shook my head. 'I did not marry within my village or surroundings, but my marriage turned out fairly well.'

'Fairly well, is that how you define your marriage? Ali you are joking. As far as I am concerned your marriage is not "fairly well", it is faultless.'

'I think you're exaggerating. Anyway you were talking about the early days of your marriage,' I encouraged her to continue.

'It was especially difficult when I did not have my own kitchen. Cooking times were my worst nightmare. Everybody disappeared, leaving me to cook more often than everybody else. We were about eight women at the homestead, but I cooked at least four or five times a week for at least twenty people, and that excluded the neighbours who were often around at mealtimes. I simply wanted to do my own cooking, just as I had done back home. But my husband was in no hurry to build me my kitchen. "You must be patient. If we hurry, my relatives will think you don't like their food" was his usual excuse. Fortunately my father-in-law was an angel. He literally forced his son to build me my kitchen. When it was built I celebrated. I was so happy. My father-in-law was a good man. He was the only person in the house I felt comfortable talking to. Sadly none of his children seem to have taken after him.

When he died of malaria, I grieved as if I had lost my own father. I felt cheated.

'My other real problem was that I did not get pregnant immediately. That simply depressed me. I prayed every day for a baby. I was accused of having used and abused some Depo Provera contraceptives during my teenage years. They said this had apparently ruined my womb and as a result I would never have children. I did not know what they were talking about. Shange had had children already with his previous girlfriends, so automatically the fault lay with me. One day my sister-in-law Shiwa just gave it to me. My husband had not returned home to eat. I was worried. I asked her if she had any idea as to where he could be. Do you know what she said?'

I shook my head.

'*Okwa yi ku yakweni mbo haya vala!*'* Kauna said, shaking her head slowly, as if just thinking of what Shiwa had said all those years ago still stung her. 'That killed me. Can you imagine how I felt? Since then, I have never asked anybody where Shange was: I worry silently. My own mother was another headache. At my brother, Blacky's funeral, at the first chance she had to be alone with me, she asked if something had not happened yet, if I was not yet pregnant.

' "All the women who married around the same time as you, have babies now – even the ones who were married after you," she said as if she was accusing me of not getting pregnant. At the funeral people stared at me. I felt uncomfortable. Mee Fennie noticed that my sadness was caused by something more than my brother's death.

' "What is wrong child?"

' "Nothing has happened yet," I whispered through my tears,

* 'He went to those with fertile wombs!'

21

pointing at my stomach. She put her arms around my arms and allowed my head to rest on her shoulders.

' "Child, these things happen with time, and as long as you worry about what people might think, it will not happen."

' "Mother asked me why I was not pregnant. She said . . ."

' "Don't listen to your mother. You know how she is, she worries about every little thing that people say and think," Mee Fennie said, rubbing my back with her right hand. ' "You remember Mee Ndapandula?" I nodded, my head still resting on her shoulders. "She only had a baby after being married for nearly ten years. You have only just got married . . ."

' "But it is a year and some months now and nothing has happened yet," I told her, not comforted by Mee Ndapandula's ten-year story at all.

' "It will happen, just don't think too much about it," Mee Fennie assured me.

'But I knew she was promising me something over which she had no control. Still, I tried not to worry, not to think too much. It was hard, very hard. Every time I felt my stomach moving or missed my period or just did not feel well, I thought, maybe this is it! Those were tough years. Then one day the miracle happened. I almost touched the sky. It took almost three years. Three long years! I would wake up in the middle of the night to feel my stomach just to make sure I was not dreaming. In the morning when I woke up my stomach was still there, growing larger every day. Until my baby was born nothing seemed real. I named her 'Kandiwapa', God I cannot thank you enough. I took her everywhere: to church, to Wednesday evening meetings, and to the women's gatherings. The women teased me and would call her 'Ondjembo yakatusha'. If she was not in my arms, she was on my back.'

'Is that why you love her more than you do your other children?'

22

'No, I love all my children equally. How can you say such a thing?' Kauna snapped at me.

'I was just asking. Don't bite my head off.'

'Enough of my stories. What about you? How were your good old days?'

'You know my story. I got married with a child already, so I didn't have to endure the accusation of ruining my womb with some Depo Provera contraceptives or whatever; and to answer your question, Michael built my kitchen quite quickly. Within one month.'

'You asked him?'

'No, no. I didn't. He said it was always best for a wife to have her own kitchen, and the sooner the better. Don't look at me like that. I tell you it was his idea. Anyway, within a month, Michael, Michael junior and I had our own kitchen. Five months later we had our own homestead.'

'Lucky you.'

'Well, I don't know but I think my husband was in more of a hurry to move away than I was. Again it was said to be my fault. I had done something to make him want to run away from his relatives. But my worst experience happened after Michael had proposed to me. I had to be "forgiven" before I could get married. I had to attend the "forgiveness" classes. I was told to make an appointment with our village pastor, Pastor Theodora. It was hell. Every time I went to his house, he was either "too busy" and couldn't see me, or away from the village. Imagine walking ten kilometres for nothing. Finally he "found time" to sit with me. He invited me to the church study. He asked me to explain why I was looking for him with such "persistence". That man was something! I looked at his face, which I thought needed shaving, and answered him.

' "Tate Pastor, I have violated the sixth commandment."

'He looked at me as if I had completely disgusted him. I felt

23

naked. After a long silence he asked me, "How did you violate the sixth commandment?" He looked at me in a funny way. It made me feel uncomfortable. I looked at the dusty religious books on the shelves and wished they would fall down and hide me from that man for good.

' "I became pregnant out of wedlock," I answered, clenching my hands together.

'He informed me that he needed the elders' council to be present. He would consult with them to find out when we could meet again. If Michael had not proposed to me, I would have died a "sinner". It is not worth the humiliation. The church elders asked a lot of personal questions. Where we did it? When we did it? How many times we did it? What did we think? And, would we do it again? There were about fifteen of us who were "forgiven". Twelve girls – three men. We had to stand in front of the congregation one Sunday for them to see us.

' "People should know that you are now forgiven, so that when they see you receiving Holy Communion, they will not have questions about your forgiveness status," Pastor Theodora explained. The church was full to capacity. All those eyes! I could have died!

'But, do you know what? God Almighty does not sleep. Barely a month after my forgiveness, Pastor Theodora's fifteen-year-old daughter became pregnant.'

'Fifteen years old?' exclaimed Kauna, shocked.

'Yes, fifteen years old, and that was not all, her *omulongi* was responsible.'

'Her what?'

'You heard me. Her own teacher! He was dismissed immediately. It was even rumoured that her mother used roots in her home-brew without success. That girl never had to attend any of those forgiveness classes. She did not appear in front of anybody. She was just forgiven. That was it!'

Kauna wondered if this was how her father treated people who needed his services.

'You said your mother-in-law accused you of bewitching her son?' she asked.

'Yes, because according to her, he loves me too much.'

'What about her daughter, what's her name again? The one who is married to Foibe's brother?'

'Oh, you mean Sana?'

'Yes, Sana.'

'She is married to Tauno.'

'Yes, Tauno, that's his name. He is a good man and treats her well. He doesn't beat her, doesn't go after other women, loves his kids and sends her goods from wherever he is working.'

'So, what does your mother-in-law say about Tauno?'

' "My daughter has a husband who loves her very much," but she doesn't say the same of me. Rather, she abuses me. "My son has a wife who has bewitched him. That woman is the laziest person I've known. Go and see for yourself. You will be confused as to whether you have entered a chicken coop, a pigsty or a homestead. *Oompambas*, *oontungwas* and chicken shit lying all over the place. It is her husband who keeps that house clean! Now that he is away at work, it is a pigsty."

'Mother-in-law does not say a word about her daughter's untidiness and her children's snotty noses and shitty buttocks. But you should hear what she has to say about me. "Oh my son, I feel so sorry for him, the woman he married, so lazy, so lazy." '

'In-laws always give their daughter-in-laws a hard time,' Kauna said.

'Especially the women, uuuh, they are worst.'

'Yes, the women.'

'The bitches.'

25

'And witches.'

'You can say that again.'

'The witches.'

'Yes, the fucking witches.'

'You are teaching me bad language,' Kauna said.

'Sometimes it's good for you.'

As we approached the pit, we saw about seven women and ten children standing around it.

'Guess who has come to fetch water,' I said to Kauna.

'Who?'

'The woman from the white house.'

'Oh, my goodness, how do I look?' Kauna asked, flattening her dress with her left hand.

'You know you are the purple violet of Oshaantu,' I responded.

Some women had already fetched their water but were just hanging around chatting with one another. I greeted each woman individually. I started with Mee Firida, a distant relative of Michael.

'*Meme Firida, wu uhala po.*'*

'*Eeee*,' she responded to my greetings as if she were singing.

'*Onawa tuu?*'†

'*Eeee.*'

'*Kegumbo oya lala po tuu?*'‡

'*Eeee.*'

Kauna followed suit. She greeted each woman in turn but ignored the woman from the white house. The children each greeted Kauna and me. The woman from the white house lifted her full calabash, balanced it on her head, swung her hips and left. The women exchanged looks. Kauna tied a rope to the

---

* 'Good day to you, Meme Firida.'
† 'Is it fine?'
‡ 'How are they all at home?'

26

handle of the bucket, dropped it down the pit and waited until it was heavy with water, then she pulled the rope up arm over arm, left right, left right until the bucket reached the surface. In the meantime, I exchanged small talk with MeFirida.

'How is everybody doing at home?'

'We are leaning towards the end that does not leak,' she responded with sudden tiredness.

'How is Tate Sebuloni doing? I heard he was not doing so well last week,' I asked after her husband.

'He was getting better but then he started working in the field. Last night I didn't sleep a wink. He was coughing, coughing the whole night. He doesn't want to listen. I keep telling him that he is not a young man any more and should no longer work in the field, especially in this cold. Do you think he listens? *Aayee*, no, he just sneaks out of the house and back to the field. Now I have to watch him like a baby who has just discovered that he can crawl,' she said, balancing her bucket on her head and getting ready to leave.

'Why did you ignore the woman from the white house?' I asked Kauna on our way home.

'Why should I greet somebody who sleeps with my husband? In fact I contemplated pushing her down the pit and covering it with a piece of rusted tin and then ordering all the women in the village not to fetch water there ever again.'

'You?'

'Yes, me.'

I laughed so loudly that the water from my bucket spilled all over my face and shoulders. Kauna laughed too.

Chapter Two

The sound of the cocks woke me up. Slowly, I opened my eyes to the darkness in the hut. Sleeping next to Kauna reminded me why I was there. I don't remember how long I stayed up last night. After I blew out the candle, I didn't fall asleep immediately. I listened to the mourners coming and going. I turned round and looked at Kauna who was still sleeping so peacefully that I couldn't help but wonder if she knew that her husband had died. I hope her strange behaviour will not continue into today, I thought.

Then I remembered whom Kauna reminded me of. She reminded me of Meme Namutenya. Something had been familiar about my friend's behaviour yesterday, some vague memory which had nagged me. Now I recalled what it was.

◆

It had all started shortly after Mee Namutenya's husband, Tate Oiva, took a second wife after more than twenty years of marriage. She came from a good family. Not wealthy but good: decent people.

According to Tate Oiva, his young wife respected Meme Namutenya as the senior wife. That impressed him. He praised her. 'You know how women are these days, fight for nothing and about every little thing. I am grateful to my wives that they get along so well,' Tate Oiva would tell people. And in the beginning, everything did go well. Meme Namutenya and

28

her husband's second wife seemed to like each other. The husband treated them 'equally'. He would, however, often give more money to the senior wife and be seen more often with her in public. The second wife did not mind. People were not altogether surprised by this 'great' relationship between the two women. Mee Namutenya was generally known to be a good person, one who was nice to everybody. She never seemed to get angry or raise her voice. She rarely went to the *cuca* shops. Those who knew the second wife from her village had similarly good things to say about her. She did not spend her time at *cuca* shops and she did not get drunk either. Her public record was almost clean, except that she had had a child with a married man, which had almost caused a divorce.

One day Mee Namutenya became sick. She was in and out of the hospital. The doctors found nothing wrong with her. She started to talk to herself. One Saturday afternoon Mee Namutenya went to Mr Jackson's *cuca* shop. Without warning she undressed herself and stood naked in front of all the men there! As naked as the day she was born. Her husband was furious and embarrassed. He took her to the hospital. She was there for a week. Again the doctors found nothing wrong with her. When she came out of hospital, she was worse than before. She kept going to the *cuca* shops, especially to Mr Jackson's, undressed herself before men and then chased after them. Her husband was advised to take her to a herbalist. This did not help either. Mee Namutenya went crazy! She became another person. She was filthy, dirty and loud. A woman of few words had turned into a person who talked non-stop. It was hard to bear. It hurt to see her. It was especially difficult for the children. Her husband returned her to her people. He claimed that he could no longer take care of her. She refused to stay with them. She would not even spend one night there. She walked the whole night and half a day and showed up at noon at Oshaantu looking for her husband.

Oiva refused to have her in his house. He warned her relatives that she was no longer under his care and that he would not be held responsible for whatever happened to her. People in the village were upset with him, especially the women. They believed that it was Mee Namutenya who had burnt the fire of wealth for him, but now that he was a rich man and she was sick, he was throwing her out like a piece of broken old pot. Some people actually accused him of using the *muti* to kill her, so that he could be with his second wife. But instead the *muti* made her crazy. Despite the fact that the second wife nursed Mee Namutenya and took care of her children, she was also accused of bewitching her. Rumours had it that she did not want to share Tate Oiva with his wife. The herbalist even assured those who paid to hear who had bewitched Mee Namutenya that 'It was the husband's second wife!' Some of us were very angry with the second wife. We did not talk to her. We ignored her and refused her in our social circles. Some women made it their personal business to make her life hell in Oshaantu. We mourned Mee Namutenya's condition. It was as if she had died. Today, Mee Namutenya lives where she can: in the bushes, at people's houses and just wherever she decides to spend the night. She is now one of those women. We have almost forgotten that she was ever a quiet person.

◆

Meme Sofia, Shange's cousin, prepared breakfast for Kauna and me. 'As soon as she wakes up, please let me know so that we can gather for the prayer,' she requested me after we had exchanged greetings. Kauna looked a little better. It seemed as if her previous hysteria had left her. But she did not want to eat.

'You did not want to eat anything yesterday. You must eat, Kauna. Don't do this to yourself,' I told her, but she made no attempt to eat.

'Yesterday . . .' she said. Her mouth was so dry that she seemed to have difficulty in parting her lips.

'What about yesterday?'

'Did . . . did people think I'd gone crazy?' she asked, looking at me straight in the eyes.

'Of course not, nobody thought that,' I said firmly, avoiding her stare. 'Look, don't think about yesterday now. You need to eat and get some strength. Mee Sofia said . . .'

'I heard her,' Kauna interrupted. 'Do we have to have the prayer every morning?' she asked, staring at the thatched roof.

'Not only every morning, but also every evening. You know that, don't you?'

'Yes, I know that,' Kauna said, sounding tired.

Mourners, mostly Shange's relatives, were already sitting on the ground in an open space near the entrance to the homestead, some with Bibles and hymn books. They stared at Kauna as if she were someone who had miraculously recovered from a dreadful disease that nobody expected her to survive. As soon as Kandiwapa saw her mother she started to cry. Kauna and I also sat on the ground. Her two-year-old son, Shopi, came and sat on her lap and she cradled him protectively in her arms. Her other four children sat beside her. My heart went out to them. Tate Mbenjameni read from the Bible, prayed and suggested a song. We sang three more songs and thus concluded the first morning prayer. Mourners greeted Kauna and expressed their sympathy. We returned to the hut.

I spent the rest of the day attending to people who came to

express their sympathy. Some were genuine; others, I thought, just curious.

Shange's relatives came pouring in until late in the afternoon. They arrived in small and large groups. Depending on who was there, the mourners would start crying all over again. 'Poverty, poverty, wuu, wuu, wuu, poverty has befallen us. My pillar, my pillar is gone,' they cried out loud. Every time somebody referred to Shange's homestead as *oshigumbo* and not *egumbo*, I was reminded that Shange had really died.

Mr Jackson, a teacher at the local primary school and a close friend of Shange's, was very helpful in arranging for the body to be transported to Onandjokwe hospital; and he drove to Oshakati to have the death of Shange announced on national radio, so that both Shange's and Kauna's family and acquaintances would hear the sad news. It turned out, however, that some of Shange's relatives were upset with Mr Jackson because he did not mention their names when he made the radio announcement.

'I did not leave out your names intentionally. The producer would not let me talk for long enough to mention everyone's name. Plus, if I had mentioned everybody's name, everyone who is related to or knows Shange, no other callers would have had a chance to call in and give their own important messages,' Mr Jackson tried to explain.

'But still you left out some of the uncles who were very important to Shange, uncles who had slaughtered a lot of cows at his wedding and who will do so in this case. That was not good at all,' one woman complained. Mr Jackson sighed.

'This is not the first time that the Shanges have done this sort of thing and ignored some relatives,' another man added. Mr Jackson shook his head.

'Look here, people. I am here because of my friend Shange. I don't even know some of you. Why would I deliberately leave your names out?' He was on the verge of losing his temper. 'I have no business with anybody here. I simply came to bury Shange, my friend. That is all. I brought my own blanket and my own food.'

'Besides, *Miitiri*, it is not your fault that our names were not mentioned. You are right, you don't know us,' another relative, also a teacher, said soothingly. Mr Jackson dropped his shoulders, clearly frustrated. His short, stout body was dripping with sweat.

◆

From Kauna's hut we listened to everything that was going on in the homestead. Occasionally I would whisper to her who I thought had arrived. Sad occasion as it was supposed to be, it was also one where relatives, friends and acquaintances who had not seen one another for years met again. For relatives, it was like a family reunion. As they arrived they would hug, kiss and cry.

Kauna and I made ourselves comfortable on the floor on a straw mat and she leant against the bed.

'I still don't understand how he died, just like that. He was not sick. I don't remember him complaining about any illness. Why would he just die?' Kauna asked.

'Only a doctor or nurse can answer those questions. Try not to think too much about it,' I said.

'Why did he die, just like that? Why did he die here? Here at home? Now people will suspect me,' Kauna asked over and over again, as if to relieve her heavy heart.

'It doesn't matter where and how he died, you would be still suspect number one.'

'Ya, you're right.' She gave a long sigh. Suddenly she turned around.

'Do you think the woman from the white house has anything

to do with this, so as to make me look bad?' Kauna asked, lowering her voice. It was odd that under these circumstances she would still refer to the other woman as the woman from the white house.

'I've thought of that possibility too, but why would she do anything like that? She is pregnant.'

'Pregnant? Pregnant again?'

'Oh, you didn't know? I thought you knew.'

'No, I didn't know. My goodness! Now they will say I was jealous of his girlfriend and bewitched him. Oh, my God, what is happening to me?'

I felt like cutting my tongue into a thousand pieces. I looked at her feeling so sad.

'Listen, don't worry, try not to think about that woman. Try to rest. I will be here for you,' I said, not sure if I was saying the right thing. Kauna got up from the floor and lay on the bed. Although the hysteria of yesterday had left her, there was still a side of Kauna emerging that I did not know.

◆

Who would have thought last Sunday that this was how we would spend our next Sunday?

Kauna had invited me to go to church with her. 'You truly are the child of a pastor,' I remarked when I agreed to do so. When I decline her invitation, she goes with her children or alone. Going to church all by herself is something she does not seem to mind doing. When my husband is at home, I go with him. He is like Kauna, he doesn't like to miss church.

Once there I was happy that I had agreed to accompany her; the choirs sang beautifully. We sat in two separate rows. The women were in the right wing of the church and the men in the left with just a few exceptions. The children sat in a separate row to the left of the altar. When the church is full, adults make the children sit on the floor. As usual, Mee Maita was there, dressed more conservatively than the rest of us and frequenting the altar more than the pastor. Her 'reading glasses' looked as if they were intended more for her nose than her eyes.

She is one of the church elders who has the responsibility of starting the hymns. As a result she sings louder than everybody else. She does a good job decorating the altar: white tablecloths with crosses embroidered in purple or green create a somewhat holy sight. The image of Jesus Christ as a white man with long blond hair and a crown of thorns around his head hangs in front of the altar.

Pastor Hallao ascended to the pulpit. This man is handsome, I thought as I looked at our young pastor. He is new and so different from all the others I have known. His outfits and haircuts are in the latest fashion. I enjoy his preaching. Short, straight to the point and relevant to our daily lives. He is more lenient with the appearance of women than the old retired Pastor Shoopala. Pastor Hallao allows women to dress as they wish and paint their faces with as many colours as they want: red lips, blue eyelids, pink cheeks, black dots on noses and foreheads. However they want to decorate their faces is fine by him. As long as they come to church, participate in church activities and make their financial contributions, he is happy. But the old retired pastor, whoooo! For him such behaviour was witchcraft in daylight. He considered their appearance an abomination and assured those women that there was no place for them in the Kingdom of God. Pastor Shoopala almost had a heart attack when he saw how liberal the young man was. Pastor Hallao, drawing on his seven years in Europe, would tell Pastor Shoopala that the people who brought the Bible to this region painted their faces, wore jewellery on their noses and put on whatever they felt comfortable in when they went to church. 'If they don't see anything wrong with that, why should we? Go to Europe and see for yourself,' he would challenge his colleague.

We simply love him.

The offering period is such a relief. Time to stretch our legs and move around a little bit. Just sitting feels as if it will kill me sometimes. Holding my hymn book and singing, I followed Kauna to the altar where the basket for the offering lay. My eyes caught a few familiar faces as I walked back to my seat. Sitting down again, I could clearly see who was in church wearing what and who comes to church regularly. Holding my hymnal in both hands, I glanced at the people in front of us. When certain familiar faces passed by, we exchanged smiles; with others I decided to concentrate on my book. Here and there I would lose my lines and just mumble the words. On Sundays, the normal appearance of many churchgoers changes. It is hard to imagine that these are the same people we see during the week. Their dirty, sometimes torn, clothes are replaced with beautiful outfits. The hard cracks in our heels are well hidden by shoes. The familiar sight of half-naked children is transformed by their clothes, though they usually cannot wait to get home to abandon them. Church attire contrasts the haves and have-nots. Teachers and nurses usually stand out. They wear hats and shoes that match their expensive outfits. Occasionally some of us are mistaken for being teachers and nurses when we have put on our best finery.

The service had long been concluded, but people were still talking and making announcements that had nothing to do with church matters: a meeting for a political party, the schedule for the pension points, somebody's husband has visited after an absence of over a year, mothers are reminded to take their babies to the local schools, clinics and traditional courts as the mobile team from the big hospital is coming to immunise children, and so on. The aftermath of the service becomes a village free-for-all. This is what discourages me from going to church. People like to talk! It is only the singing that really keeps me going through the service. If there is a wedding, baptism, confirmation, forgiveness or any of those church rituals, I stay in bed 'sick' unless I have a direct role to play in them. Kauna must have noticed my restlessness.

'Please be patient, these are important messages,' she said.

'What?'

'Later.' She indicated silence with the palm of her hand.

◆

But this Sunday everything is different.

After church, some people came to express their sympathy to the relatives. They say Shange's death was announced after the service. I thought of my husband and wondered if he had heard the news on the radio. It is almost two months since he has written to us. I wondered what he would think and whether he would come to Shange's funeral.

What will happen to me and to our children if my husband dies? I don't like to think about it, but sometimes I can't help it. Maybe it will be better if I die first. Michael will not neglect the children, and he will probably marry another woman. But I don't want to die and I don't want my husband to die. I pray that God will keep us both until our children have finished school and are old enough to take care of themselves, and I pray for our daughter to find a good husband. I pray for Michael's safety too. 'If you pray for me, I will be fine,' he assures me. But I worry about him all the time, especially since that terrible minibus accident three years ago.

'I don't remember the details of the accident as I was sleeping,' Michael recounted the incident when I visited him at the

37

Oshakati hospital. 'It was God's divine protection that this was so. Our people don't care about us, my dear wife. All they care about is making money. A sixteen-seat minibus had twenty-eight people on board. It was full to capacity but still the driver kept allowing more people in and loading on more luggage. We were packed like small fishes in a tin. At Otjiwarongo, I thought of getting off and I wish I had done so. Eleven people died in that accident. Can you imagine that so many people died for nothing? People who were looking forward to being with their friends and loved ones died because others were greedy. It was just by God's mercy that some of us survived with broken legs and ribs. It was a nightmare. That accident really taught me about the value of life and what people will do for money.'

I left my children in the care of Kauna and my mother-in-law. I stayed at the Oshakati hospital for over a month caring for my husband. A friendly woman who was looking after her son allowed me to share her open hut. I slept on the cold cement floor and prayed day and night that my husband would live.

◆

During the afternoon I went to look for Sustera, the local nurse. I was told she was not back from a wedding. I was disappointed. The sun was sinking and it was getting dark when I entered the house of mourning.

Meme Katilina, one of the neighbours, hurried toward me and unexpectedly grabbed my upper left arm. 'I need to talk to you,' she whispered so urgently that I felt her warm breath on my face.

'Listen, child, we need to put all Kauna's things together and lock them up in a room or take them somewhere to a place where they will be safe,' she said, her eyes wide with fear. I did not understand what she meant.

'Don't look so confused, we must hide all her things.'

'I don't know if that is such a good idea,' I said.

'What do you mean, you don't know if that is such a good idea? I am talking about your friend, and if you are her true friend and are concerned about her and her children's well-being, you won't tell me you are not sure.'

'Well, I mean I don't know how Kauna will feel about this . . . I am not sure if she wants to fight over property.'

'Who talked about fighting over property? I am talking about protecting *her* property, *her property*, child,' she said, squeezing my arm. I pulled back and she let go. 'Besides, do you think that child is in any position to take care of her things? So, in this case, you are the person who should take care of her goods,' she went on. I rubbed my arm where she had gripped me.

'You should make the decisions for her,' she continued. 'You are her friend. You cannot allow these people to take away her belongings. She will not get anything from her husband's property, so why do you want her to lose her own as well? You know how few rights we have around here, especially after the death of a husband. His relatives always have more rights.' She pinned my arms against my side in her anxiety. I looked at her frowning and she released them.

'Look, child, I saw things happening last night and this is why I am talking to you. I am not just trying to be nosy. I suspect that this child friend of yours has already lost all her animals,' she said, pleased that I was finally listening. 'Last night my friend Mee Johanna, Nelago's mother, you know Nelago, the one . . .'

'Yes, yes I know her,' I cut her short.

'OK,' she said, pleased that I knew whom she was talking about.

'We were going to the bathroom. As we approached the kraal, we heard men in this loud argument. We stopped to listen to what was going on. Of course, we did not mean to listen in. Child, you know me better than that. Anyway, the argument sounded more like a fight, so we had to wait and see if it was safe for us to go to the bathroom. My child, my child, it was the whole bunch, the Shanges. The brothers, cousins, nephews, uncles, grandfathers, you name them. They were all there, old and young. They were fighting over cattle. Some animals were already being driven away. It's just that my sight is failing me these days,' she said, rubbing her eyes. 'I couldn't see exactly who drove the cattle away and how many were being driven away. But I know it was the Shanges, the whole lot.

' "That is my bull, that is my bull, yeyeyeye, yeyeyeye . . ."

' "No, that is not your bull . . ."

' "Yes, that is not your bull . . ."

' "Yes, it is my bull. *Nakusa* promised me this bull. Ask Mee Kauna, she knows everything. If you don't believe me, go and ask her. Go, she is in the house. Go and ask her. She too knows how much *Nakusa* and I talked about this bull and how much I loved it."

' "You are such a liar. How did *Nakusa* know you loved this bull? You two did not even talk to each other."

' "Don't call me a liar, don't call me a liar, I warn you."

' "Hey, don't push me."

' "Take your filthy hands off my brother's cattle. You are not even a relative, you greedy old goat."

' "Don't insult my father. We have every right to be here and to inherit. If you don't know the history of your relatives, shut up!"

' "People, people, why don't you bring all the animals together so that they can be divided equally among the relatives and the children."

' "Whose children?"

' "Eh, whose children, Mr Jackson? And why don't you stay out of this? You are not a relative. What are you doing here anyway? This is family business."

'Driving their "inheritance" away, they disappeared into the bush and into the darkness.'

Mee Katilina told me the story with so much animation that it sounded like a folk tale. 'That was terrible, terrible. This inheritance thing. I don't know where it will lead us, I am sure they took all her animals. You must go and find out what they have taken and report it to her people when they arrive.'

I didn't know what to say to that old woman. I was not sure if I wanted to be involved in Kauna and her dead husband's property wrangles, and her Christian background made things more complicated still. But I also knew that unless I gave Mee Katilina a satisfactory answer, she would not stop bothering me.

'I don't think Kauna has lost anything yet. She did not have many animals. Maybe a few goats and two or three pigs,' I explained.

'Kauna did not have animals? Didn't she come with her own animals? I am sure her uncles did not send her empty-handed, just like that, without anything – cows, goats, nothing?' she asked with her arms firmly crossed.

Then I tried to put the onus on Shange. 'I think Shange discouraged her from owning animals,' I answered, hoping I was not saying too much.

'Oh my God, what an awful man that Shange child was!' she said with a disgusted expression on her face.

As strong Christians, Kauna's parents believed that taking

41

cattle with her, as most other brides would, could negatively affect their marriage. 'A wealthy bride is not good for a husband's ego' is what Kauna's mother apparently said. However, I left out this piece of information.

'But I hope her husband's attitude did not prevent Kauna from keeping animals at other people's houses. At her friends' houses perhaps.' She looked at me as if I were supposed to know what she was talking about.

'No, no, no, Mee Katilina, Kauna was not into that sort of a thing. Don't even raise that as a possibility.' I dismissed her statement.

'It was just an idea, women do that you know, if the husband . . .'

'Well, Meme, let me go to Kauna, she must be wondering what has happened to me,' I interrupted her.

'Let me come along and hear what Kauna has to say about this. Let me see how I can help,' she said and started to walk ahead of me.

Afraid to be implicated in some 'inheritance hunt', I lied. 'Actually Kauna is not well. This is why I went to look for Sustera. As soon as I find out how she is doing, I will come and talk to you,' I said, holding her back with both my hands.

When I got to the hut, Kauna was with kuku Hilma, Mee Aune and another woman whose name I didn't remember. They all sat on the floor. We exchanged greetings and they stood up to leave.

'Did I chase you away?' I asked them lightly.

'Oh no, child, we had already said good night to Kauna just before you arrived,' kuku Hilma said, and they left.

'More people coming to express their sympathy, eh?' I remarked to Kauna.

'Yes, it was pleasant to have these ones with me. They shared a few encouraging words. It was nice,' she said, yawning.

42

'Sustera is not back yet from the weekend. I will try tomorrow.'

I decided not to tell her about the alleged fighting over cattle at the kraal. There would be time to do so.

Chapter Three

Mee Fudheni, the soft-spoken nurse at the local clinic who is commonly known as Sustera, came to look for me at the mourning house. She arrived shortly after the early prayers and apologised for her absence over the weekend. 'I am sorry I was not here when you needed me. I will arrange with my colleague so that we are not both out of the village at the same time during weekends,' she said. 'You want me to check on Kauna . . . ?'

'Yes, Sustera,' I replied and quickly briefed her about what had taken place on Saturday. Then I led her to Kauna's hut.

Sustera sat beside Kauna on the bed and, taking her hands in her own, expressed sympathy in her usual friendly manner. Her white uniform made her look angelic. The purple epaulette on each shoulder with its three stars was the sign of a registered nurse and an educated woman. This is when I wish I was educated too, I thought as I looked at her. Her braids were carefully tied at the back of her head. Her whole appearance was clean and neat, as if to set an example of the hygienic standards she advocates.

'You look much better than I expected,' Sustera remarked.

'You know how this one is,' Kauna said, looking at me rather accusingly. 'I don't only look better, I feel better too.' Sustera did not say anything to that.

'Well, I only called Sustera to make sure that everything was OK with you,' I said.

'I am fine,' Kauna replied, rolling her eyes.

'Mee Ali is right, she did the right thing. With such things, stress and so on, you never know,' Sustera responded, making me feel better. She did not think I had over-reacted. 'I brought you something. It will help you to remain calm and to sleep.'

'An injection?' Kauna asked, her eyes bugged out.

'No, it is not an injection, it is just a few tablets. Take one today after you have eaten and see how you feel, but definitely take one on the day of the burial.'

'It is really not necessary,' Kauna said, pulling a face.

'Don't worry, Sustera. I will make sure she takes them.'

Sustera turned to Kauna. 'I have to return to the clinic now. The immunisation campaign is still on and you know how it is on Mondays.' She stood up, reached into her uniform pocket and brought out a small white container. 'The tablets are in here,' she said, handing me the Valium. 'I will pray for you.'

'Sustera, one more question.'

'OK.' She smiled patiently. I rubbed my hands together a couple of times before asking her.

'Sustera, how do you explain a death like this? I mean, why would a person who was not sick, did not complain of any illness and looked so healthy and strong, die just like that?'

Sustera sat down on the bed again, before answering.

'These things do happen you know. A person can, as you say, look very healthy and strong and then just drop dead without warning. We cannot always see certain life-threatening diseases that people have just by looking at them. Unless a person gets a regular medical examination, they will not be identified.'

'Life-threatening diseases such as what?' I asked with a confused frown.

'Such as high blood pressure and heart disease, especially when people are overweight . . . fat.' That surprised us.

'How can being fat cause death?'

'Yes, I know that being big is considered a sign of health and wealth and a sign of a happy marriage, especially among women,' she said with a smile. 'However, it doesn't mean the same thing in the medical profession.' Looking at our faces, Sustera realised that we didn't understand what she was telling us. She explained as simply as she could. 'When people have things wrong with them like a weak heart, which we can't see, putting strain on it by carrying a big body can make it stop just like that,' she said, snapping her fingers.

If what Sustera says is true then most women I know should be dead by now, I thought.

'Is it possible that somebody bewitched him?' I posed my question hesitantly. I almost hoped that she might not hear me.

'Well, I don't know about bewitching,' she said, trying very hard to conceal a smile. 'But if he was poisoned, the post-mortem examination will show it.' She stood up.

'Mee Kauna, with Mee Ali here beside you, you will be fine. You are very fortunate to have a friend like her. I wish I had one like her too. We are all jealous of you, you know.'

I looked at her in disbelief. I thought, she must be trying to be friendly. She wished she had a friend like me? When she left, Kauna seemed relaxed.

'Sustera is a good person,' I remarked.

'Yes, she is. She reminds me of the character Nameya in the folk tale "Queen of the River", whose very presence drove away all evil spirits," Kauna said thoughtfully.

'I thought all nurses were witches and bitches until I met Sustera.'

'I didn't think they were very nice either. Very few are as kind as she is. Usually they are so high and mighty – as if they somehow want to make you feel small or ignorant because you don't always understand modern medicine. My father always said that a good nurse saw her profession as a vocation, but so many nurses just see it as a good employment option. They don't care about their patients.'

'I agree with your father.'

'But did you hear? She said she wished she had a friend like you.'

'You think she meant that?'

'Yes, she did.'

'But she is educated . . .' I said.

'I was planning to get an education but then I got married out of school.'

'At least you got married out of high school. I did not even get that far. Mother could not afford to send me to secondary school. My father simply refused to pay my school fees despite the fact that he could have done so if he had wanted to. I think he took out the anger he felt for my mother – after she had divorced on him – on me. On the other hand, maybe I wouldn't have met Michael if I had gone to a secondary school. I would have had to board because the school was so far away. So, perhaps it was a good thing. And now we can try to make sure that our children get an education.'

'Yes, we can. But now . . .' she threw her arms apart, 'I just don't know about mine.'

Chapter Four

First they said it was the shock. 'You know some people are like that. When they're in shock, they don't cry. But once they come to terms with reality, they act differently,' one of the mourners remarked. The first day she did not cry, the second day she did not cry, the third day she did not cry and still, today, the fourth day, she had not cried. Mourners were getting tired. Rumours that Kauna was not crying or showing any emotion towards the sudden death of her husband spread like wild fire. People started to whisper and Shange's relatives got mad.

Over the past hour Kauna has done half a dozen things. She took her Bible, read a few verses to herself and put it back on the box. Changed her clothes. Took a piece of *oshithima*, lunch that was served an hour ago, which she had not eaten. She attempted to sweep the room. I stopped her. She lay on the bed staring at the roof. In the nicest and most sensitive way possible, I tried to convey the rumour to her. I cleared my throat.

'Kauna . . .'

'Mmmm.'

'There is a rumour that apparently you are not behaving like a widow . . . That you are not mourning the death of your husband . . . You are not crying . . . No tears . . . Your face is so dry that some people say they are embarrassed.' This is the worst news I have ever conveyed to anybody, I thought. 'People think you are glad he is dead . . . They think that is why you are not crying . . . They think . . .'

'But what do you think?'

'What do I think?'

'Yes, Ali, what do you think?' Kauna asked and turned on her stomach, lifting her head and supporting her chin with her right palm. She looked at me, waiting for an answer. The question caught me by surprise.

'Well, I know that Shange was not the best husband . . . most people around here know that, but your behaviour . . . It is as if you don't care.' She sat upright on the bed and crossed her legs like someone meditating. 'I am worried about the children. Aren't you?' I asked.

'Well, I'm sorry you all feel uncomfortable about my behaviour, but I cannot pretend,' she shook her head. 'I cannot lie to myself and to everybody else in this village. They all know how I was treated in my marriage. Why should I cry? For what? For my broken ribs? For my baby, the one he killed inside me while beating me? For cheating on me so publicly? For what? For what, Ali?'

For the homestead, I thought. Kauna asked all these questions with her palms open as if she begged for my understanding.

'I know all that, but I just want you to see that . . .'

'What do you want, Ali? You want to see me rattling in the sand like a snake pretending to be devastated by Shange's death?'

'I'm not saying you must pretend, all I'm trying to say is that you should also think of the rest of us: your children, relatives and friends. Your behaviour is affecting all of us,' I said, almost raising my voice as I tried to talk some sense into her. She sighed. 'Even if you hated him, do not behave as if you want the world to know that you are happy he is dead. If you do this, you will give people reasons to accuse you of being responsible for his death.'

'I thought you would understand. I thought you really would, but obviously you don't.'

49

'Oh, Kauna, how *can* you say that!' I called out, feeling terribly hurt.

'I am sorry, Ali, I did not mean that . . .'

'Look, I don't expect you to act as if you are heartbroken or anything of that sort, but death is death. A human being is dead and your children will grow up without a father.'

'It is just that those who want to see me crying will be the first to accuse me of being a hypocrite.'

'I know, my dear, but think about the children, and yourself.'

'I have been angry my whole life. I have been angry about this marriage and with this man, so at this stage I really don't think I care what happens to me if I don't cry for him. I really don't care. I have nothing to lose.'

'What about the children?' I asked.

'You know what they say about the children. "A man's children are not his; his nephews and nieces are." Don't you know that story?'

'Well, yes, but not all men believe that.'

'You mean Michael doesn't believe it.'

'Kauna, do you really want your children to grow up knowing that their mother hated their father so much that she did not shed one tear for him when he died, because she was so happy? Do you also want them to hate him? Is that what you want? It's very true that he was not nice to you, but he provided very well for his children.'

Still Kauna did not cry or show any emotion or sorrow. Rather she looked withdrawn and tired. She is not someone who cries easily – she did not even cry when her husband beat her severely. But where did this strength come from? I don't know her, I thought as I looked at her and realised that Shange would not receive a drop of her tears. When I thought of how Shange treated Kauna, I understood her reaction. He controlled and virtually ruled her life. He decided whom she should befriend and when she could visit her relatives and friends. I cried many nights for her. I always wanted her suffering to end, but I never imagined that it would happen this way. Nobody needed to die.

◆

I never understood why Shange and Kauna had ever married in the first place. They were like day and night. Two such different human beings. 'I was the daughter of a pastor and a teacher, a high school girl and a virgin. I was perfect for him. It was more for his ego than anything else. I realised that later,' Kauna told me one day. 'He worked at the mine. You know how impressive mineworkers are. And before I knew it, I was married,' she said, as if it was a joke.

I had heard it was a big wedding, bigger than the village had ever seen before, a fancy, flashy wedding. Her mother, Mee Maria, preened herself like a big bird. But as soon as Shange built their own homestead, he changed.

What I still did not understand was the way people in this community treated her. It was as if the failure of their marriage was her fault! They laughed at her and stigmatised her.

It was her fault that her husband looked at other women.

It was her fault that her husband beat her.

It was her fault that her husband did this or did that. Oh, it was just too much.

Kauna started to say, 'Maybe if I had been a nurse, a teacher or any of those office workers, he would have treated me better. Maybe if, maybe if . . .'

Chapter Five

As I sat in the room with Kauna, all sorts of things came back
to me. I remembered a weekend – it must have been about two
years ago – which had felt like one of the longest weekends of
my life. Michael and I had been to the wedding of one of his
nephews, and there I discovered something very interesting. I
couldn't wait to get back home and see Kauna. I was on
tenterhooks waiting to share my juicy story with her. And the
first thing I did when I arrived home was call my daughter,
Kauna.

'Dear, go to your *mbushe* and ask her to come and see me
now.' My daughter, sensing the urgency of the matter, rushed
off to call her namesake, but I called her back again.

'*Ila, ila*, come here, come here.' With children one never
knows. I bent down and whispered in her small ear. 'See if Tate
Shange is there first. If he is there, pretend you only went to say
halloo to your *mbushe*. If he is not there, that is when you will
give her my message. OK?' I asked, tapping her on her
shoulders.

'I will do so,' she responded, understanding quite clearly the
conspiratorial relationship between Kauna and me.

'That is my only girl. Now go!' I felt a little uneasy that I was
teaching my daughter to be really 'chicky', but I felt it couldn't
be helped. Every woman needs to learn to be cautious.

She came back very quickly and I was disappointed to hear
that Kauna was not yet back from church.

'This church thing, can't she miss church just one Sunday?' I thought out loud.

'Why this sudden need to see Mee Kauna today? What are you up to?' my husband asked. Oops! I had completely forgotten about him.

'Oh, it's nothing, eh nothing. I need to return her beads.'

'Her beads?'

'Yes, yes, her beads,' I lied through my teeth.

'You must have your own things, it is not always good to borrow.'

'I know. I know. I will send for mine from Oshakati tomorrow,' I said, feeling hot all of a sudden and itching under my armpits and in my private parts. What was I thinking, beads?

Kauna received the news that I was looking for her completely back to front. Her children had given her the impression that something had happened to me.

'I heard you were looking for me all day. Is something wrong?' she asked, out of breath and concerned.

'I'm sorry, I did not mean to scare you. Nothing is wrong. I have news for you. News that cannot wait. Let's go outside, Michael may hear us.' Holding her left hand, I led her out of the homestead, past the *mahangu* crop to the edge of the field, and sat under the *omuye* tree. 'Nobody can hear us here,' I said. 'You know what?'

'No, I don't know,' Kauna said, rather disappointed that I had worried her for nothing. At the same time, she looked curiously at the Bible in my hand.

'Guess! Where does your husband work?'

'At the mine, of course. Is that the news you have for me?'

'No, no, wait. It's coming. Be patient. Yes, he works at the mine, but what does he do?'

'Well, I don't know, I think he works with diamonds, something of that sort,' she said with a frown on her face.

53

'In the kitchen, Mama, in the kitchen.'

'In the kitchen? What kitchen? Doing what in the kitchen?'

'Yes, in the kitchen, the mine kitchen, cooking in the kitchen.'

'No? Cooking for who?'

'Yes, cooking for the other men there.'

'No, no, I don't believe this.'

'Yes.'

'Yes, I knew you wouldn't believe it. He cooks for them, feeds them, washes the dishes, cleans the pots, the kitchen and does all that kitchen work.'

'Shange . . . ?'

'Let me show you something.' I reached for the Bible and took out a picture. For a moment she looked as if she did not recognise the person in the photograph. She frowned.

'It is my husband,' she said at last.

'Yes, it is your husband.'

The picture showed Shange wearing a blue overall and a white apron. He had a white hat on his head. In the background was a huge black stove against which he was leaning. Everything in the picture seemed so gigantic: huge pots, knives, spoons and forks.

'I don't believe this,' Kauna said softly, wiping the photograph with her right hand.

'Well, seeing is believing,' I replied. 'Can you imagine Shange working in a kitchen . . . ?' Kauna handed me the photo so suddenly it fell to the ground.

'Sorry,' she said.

'Are you OK?' I asked her when I realised that she had fallen very quiet.

'Yes . . . I am . . .' she said, looking intent. 'Where did you get that picture anyway?'

'It was in an album at the wedding. The owner of the album knows Shange very well. I don't remember the fellow's name, but they worked together in the kitchen. He said they are called "chefs" not cooks and, apparently, they are trained in the capital. And they say your husband is a great cook,' I tickled her on her side. She did not laugh.

'And you stole the picture,' said Kauna rather accusingly.

'No, I did not steal it. I brought it to show you. What is wrong with you anyway?'

Kauna thought about how her husband had talked about the mine and the image of him she had created in her mind. Nothing about it conformed with the faded photograph. Then the familiar sound of a car made us both turn our heads.

'It is your husband.'

'Did he see us?'

'I don't think so.'

'He is only returning now from the white house. He left on Friday.'

'Since Friday?'

'Ya, you know how he is with that woman. I think she had peed in his food. I must chop it off and put it in my purse for safekeeping.'

'Kauna!'

'It's a joke,' she said. 'I need to go home.'

'Yes, let me see you off.'

As we passed our homestead, we almost bumped into my husband. I quickly gave the Bible to Kauna. My husband and Kauna exchanged greetings.

'How was church today?' Michael asked Kauna, looking at the Bible.

'With the forgiveness ceremony, it took forever.'

'Oh yes, that's right.'

'My husband is now home, I will visit you properly some other time,' she said and left.

'Greet him for me,' Michael said. He gave me a suspicious look. I avoided his stare. When our husbands were around, Kauna and I didn't spend as much time together as we wanted to.

I was a bit disappointed at her reaction. I thought we were going to scream with laughter. She was not as surprised or amused as I thought she would be. It was almost as if she was disappointed to see the picture. Could it be that Shange's lowly status was just another blow to her pride? I had not thought of this. Maybe it was not such a juicy story after all.

Kauna took the Bible to her hut. The picture would be safe there. Shange never went into her hut. She went to look for Shange in the living room, his favourite place. Their house consisted of a bedroom, a kitchen and a living room. He was sitting in his favourite chair, smoking his cigarette and rocking himself. Husband and wife exchanged greetings.

'Are you OK?' Shange asked with a suspicious frown on his face.

'Yes yes. Yes, I am OK,' Kauna responded quickly.

'So why are you looking at me like that?'

'Looking at you?'

'Yes, looking at me.'

'Can't I look at my husband without being challenged?'

'No no no no no,' he said, shaking his head. 'Don't give me that. What is that look in your eyes for?'

'I miss you.'

'Please, Kauna, don't push me too far. Your husband doesn't sleep at home for the entire weekend and you tell him that you miss him? What is on your mind? Are you planning to poison me?'

'Oh, Tate Shange, how can you say that?'

'Don't "Oh, Tate Shange" me. I don't trust you. I have been married to you for fourteen years and I have never seen anything like the look you now have on your face. Whatever it is, I will find out and if it is poison, I will know that Ali gave it to you.'

Chapter Six

Maybe I shouldn't have shown Kauna the picture of her husband taken in a mine kitchen. Or maybe I should have just kept the picture to myself, or shouldn't have brought it from the wedding in the first place. As it happened, Kauna's third son, Kangulu, discovered the photograph. He thought his father with the big hat and white apron was very funny. Shange had never seen the photo before, but he recognised himself. He asked his son to show him where he had found it. In his mother's hut. Who gave it to her and how long had she had it? he thought as he scrutinised his own photograph. Shange couldn't understand his feelings. Was he embarrassed or angry? He was irritated. He started to fume and couldn't wait for Kauna to return from the well. Then it all happened so fast. Kauna and her basket full of water landed on the ground. Kauna tried to escape Shange's rage, but he was too fast for her. He caught her. She screamed. I have never heard her screaming like that.

'It is Kauna!' I called out. Without wasting time, Michael took off to the Shanges' homestead.

'Shange, stop it! Stop it! I said stop it!' Michael shouted at Shange to let go of his wife. 'Shange, I said stop it! What is wrong with you? Stop it!' Michael yelled again. Kauna was lying on the ground covered in a blanket of sand. She moved like an old cloth as Shange's shoes struck her mercilessly all over her tiny body. The heavy mine shoes sounded as if they were breaking every bone. She had covered her face and part of her head with both her arms and hands. Michael held Shange from behind his back in an effort to pull him away. Kauna, supporting herself on all fours, bravely tried to stand up, when Shange suddenly pushed Michael away with both his elbows. Michael staggered backwards, lost balance and landed on the ground. Shange, freed from Michael's grip, rushed to Kauna who was crawling like a newborn calf and kicked her hard in the stomach. She flew into the air and fell on the ground. Michael regained his balance and held Shange tight, clinging to the man as if Kauna's life depended on that grip. Holding the extremely reluctant Shange from behind, Michael slowly pushed him to their three-bedroomed concrete house. Shange did not utter a single word. His face gleamed with sweat and anger. He breathed like a wounded animal.

I will remember this sight of Kauna for as long as I live. Blood mixed with sand all over her face, in her mouth, nose, eyes, ears, head and clothes, and the sight of her children crying helplessly. 'Oooh!' called out the onlookers, awoken from their state of shock. I ran to Kauna and knelt beside her.

'*Omumwandje* . . .' I cried out.

'Eeeh,' she groaned in intense pain.

'Let me help you up.'

'Eeeh,' she groaned again.

'You will be fine, Kauna, you will be fine,' I whispered as consolingly as I could, finding few words to ease her pain and humiliation. One of the onlookers, realising that I needed help, came to my assistance; then two more. Kauna's eldest daughter, the eleven-year-old Kandiwapa, who was crying at the top of her voice, ran in to give me a hand. Carefully, we carried Kauna to her hut and laid her on the bed.

'I think with Kandiwapa and the other children, we will manage. Thank you very much,' I said, trying to get rid of the curious villagers. What were they looking at anyway? I thought, upset.

I boiled water and cleaned Kauna. I removed most of the sand from her face, eyes, nose and ears. Then I gently removed the sand from around the mouth: there was an ugly cut, which made me gasp and Kandiwapa cry even more pitifully. I didn't wash Kauna's hair, I just loosened the braids and brushed the sand out of it.

We heard the slam of the door. Kandiwapa and I both stood still. Minutes later we heard the sound of the vehicle being driven violently away. Shange had left. What is wrong with this man? Why did he beat her like this? I will never talk to him again, never, ever, I swear to my living parents! I thought angrily, trying very hard to hold back my tears. Occasionally Kandiwapa would give me a disapproving look when her mother groaned.

'I have to do this, *Sheeli*, otherwise she will not heal quickly. And you must stop crying now. You need to be strong for your little brothers and sisters,' I said to Kandiwapa, who had not stopped her endless whimpering.

'I will go to look for Sustera to come and examine your mother and show you how you can treat her bruises.'

'I know how to do it!' she said defensively.

'How do you know how to do it?' I asked innocently.

'I do it every time he beats her.'

'This time . . . it was worse?'

'Yes,' she said, squeezing the cloth in her hand so that the mixture of blood and water poured through her clenched fists down her tiny arm to her elbow.

'Come here,' I said. I pulled her against me and embraced her. She cried uncontrollably. Tears that told me that this little girl had seen much too much for her age.

'*Sheeli*, you know you need to be strong for your brothers

and sisters,' I said again, drying her tears with my blouse. She nodded.

I would usually discover that Shange had beaten Kauna when I noticed a bruise or when, weeks later, she mentioned it in conversation.

'Why didn't you tell me?' I would ask in shock and dismay.

'You get so angry, so emotional. I don't want to involve you in my problems to that extent.'

When Sustera saw Kauna's condition, she was upset by my feeble attempts at playing doctor. 'She needs to go to the hospital, immediately,' she instructed, indicating that things were much more serious than they looked. She asked for a car to take Kauna to Onandjokwe hospital, about eighty kilometres away. When I got home later in the afternoon, I expected Michael to talk about the incident. He didn't. He wanted to be alone.

I left the cooking to the children and took a walk in the *mahangu* field, wandering down the narrow paths to ease my own restlessness. Why had Shange done such a thing? What had got into him? He had behaved like a man possessed. I walked on. The moon had appeared already. It was just another night.

I visited Kauna at the hospital as often as I could. The nurses were not always sympathetic. In our presence they would talk about how village women get beaten up by their husbands; and how they lie to the doctors, saying that some cow had kicked them in their faces while they were milking; and that treating these women was a waste of time because they always return, worse!

◆

About twenty *cuca* shops were at Oshaantu village, half a kilometre away from the church, school and clinic. The majority of them were built with corrugated iron sheets. Two or three were made with mud. Mr Jackson's *cuca* shop was the only one built with concrete. It was painted a bright yellow with three black stripes above the two front windows. Some *cuca* shops stood in orderly rows; others stood by themselves. All *cuca* shop owners sold alcohol, either homemade or western, or both. Others sold groceries in addition to alcohol. When the people of Oshaantu are not working in their fields, the *cuca* shops are their favourite places for socialising. Mr Jackson's *cuca* shop was where the élite, the educated and visitors to the village relaxed.

It was late in the afternoon, an afternoon just like any other for Shange, enjoying his day with friends in the shade of the blue-and-red striped awning attached to Mr Jackson's *cuca* shop. Shange was oblivious to what was in store for him. He bought *tombo* for three women in exchange for a dance and singing performance to entertain him and his friends.

Mukwankala, an elderly lady well known for speaking her mind, was someone on whom women often depended to speak on their behalf. Having found Shange, she walked straight up to him, ignoring everybody else. That alerted Mr Jackson's customers. Mukwankala was not known to disregard this extremely important aspect of the local culture, the greetings. No, she was not that rude. Something was wrong.

'I heard you beat her again and this time I heard you almost killed her,' she said coldly and with contempt. It was clear to everyone that Mukwankala was on the warpath. 'Why did you beat the child like that? If you don't want her any more, why don't you send her back to her parents, because whatever she is doing, you don't seem to beat it out of her?' She looked him up and down, from head to toe. 'Have you ever looked at yourself, your body, your weight, your height?' she asked, as if it were possible that he had forgotten these things. 'How do you feel when you beat a person who cannot beat you back? How do you feel afterwards?

'Do you know that since you married that child she has not gained any weight, yet the little she has, you still want. Now, if you are such a fighter, tell me how many men have you beaten in this village the way you beat your wife? How many?' Shange looked away. 'No, not one. Yes, it is only that poor child you beat like that and I don't think she has ever lifted a finger to hurt you. Kauna cannot walk among other women with her head uplifted and straight and it is all because of you. Are you not ashamed of yourself?' Shange did not expect such a confrontation. His face turned a ghostly white.

'There is one thing that I will never understand about you. Why did you marry her in the first place? Why didn't you marry one of the many women you whored with and fathered children with? What made you think you were worthy of her? The only reason you treat her like this is because you married somebody who was undoubtedly above you. A slut should marry a slut and a decent man should marry a decent woman. If you had married a slut, you would have been the happiest man in this village.'

Shange did not say baa or boo. He did not say a word. He was as still as if he were listening to the radio. Occasionally he would look at Mukwankala and the curious villagers.

'Men who beat women are the ones who cannot stand up against other men,' Mukwankala concluded. She made us think. Shange was feared in the village, but he had never beaten anybody except his wife. His brothers beat people all the time, but Shange, no. Why was he feared if he had never beaten anybody? Any man? The curious customers stood there, holding their breaths in anticipation of the unthinkable. Her age must have saved her. Shange could have humiliated her there and then in front of everybody. But this time Shange was

63

humiliated. He wished the earth would part below him so he could disappear. Nobody made any attempt to stop Mukwankala from insulting him. Some were even quietly happy that he had been told to stop abusing his wife.

When I heard that Mukwankala had confronted Shange at the *cuca* shop, in public, I was scared to death. Although I admired her act of bravery, I thought it might cause more trouble than good. I thought that once Kauna came home, Shange would kill her.

◆

When Kauna was discharged from the hospital, a friend of Mukwankala's brought her brown shoe polish to apply to her face. 'It is good for the inside bruises and scars,' she advised and insisted that Kauna use it. Neither Kauna nor I had ever heard of shoe polish healing scars. Nevertheless, she went ahead and applied it. It burnt, burnt and burnt. It was as if her face had been put on fire! Kauna wondered if she had ever healed in the first place. 'Apply it until it doesn't burn again,' the woman advised her. Kauna applied the brown shoe polish a few more days until the burning stopped. Time is a wonderful thing. It is an ointment. It is a healer. And so it healed Kauna's wounds and bruises. However, the cut on the left corner of her upper lip left a scar that made it look bigger than the rest of her mouth. A scar that will remind us all, and particularly Kauna, of the horror of physical abuse. We were so happy when Shange returned to the mine.

'Why do you think he beat you like that?' I asked Kauna.

'Well, I don't know, I really have no idea. Usually he beats me for nothing, but this time I am not sure if it was for nothing. I did something. I am just not sure what. In the hospital I tried so hard to think of what I had done to annoy him that I gave myself a headache.' Then she looked at me as if she had suddenly remembered something. 'Your husband doesn't beat you?'

'Nooo,' I answered, totally surprised by her question.

'Has never beaten you?'

'Has never beaten me.'

'Not even a slap?'

'Not even a slap.'

'You are lucky,' she said, giving me one look and turning her back on me to face the mud wall. I said nothing. Suddenly I felt a long distance away from Kauna.

Well . . ., I thought. 'I am going home,' I said.

'Good night,' she said, as if it did not matter whether I stayed or left. From the very beginning of my relationship with Michael, people had made this kind of remark, but I had never got used to them.

'Oh, you must thank your gods, a lot of men abandon their girlfriends when they impregnate them.'

'You are very lucky, it is not always that a man marries a woman with a child, even if it is his own.'

'A man of Michael's calibre marrying an uneducated woman? Mmm, you are lucky.'

'Michael must love you . . .'

Now this. 'Oh, he doesn't beat you? You are lucky.' I am really tired of it all. Yes, Michael is a good man and I am grateful for that. I just don't know what people want me to do. Kneel down at his feet and say, 'Thank you, Michael, for marrying a low class'? I am not lucky. I simply do not deserve to be treated like a filthy animal. I gave a long sigh as I entered our homestead.

A week later Kauna brought me a hot baked *oshikwiila*. We were friends again. I asked her what she was going to do about the beating.

'Kauna, this is the very last thing I should advise you to do, but can't you leave Shange? Divorce him and go back to your parents or whatever, just to get away from him?' I asked.

'What makes you think I haven't tried?' she responded, rather surprised. 'I have left my husband about three times. The first was when we were still living with his parents. I pretended that I had gone to visit my parents. I did not say anything until Shange and his relatives turned up. The second and third times were after we had moved here. But it's always the same old story. He is sorry and will never beat me again. I just don't believe this man is the one who used to come to our house and treated us all like little princesses. My hopes for a beautiful marriage and a loving father for my children have been shattered,' Kauna said, shaking her head.

'The last time I visited Mee Fennie she gave me a lecture about divorcing Shange. "Leave him," she told me again and again. "Leave him. If you think you deserve more than what you get out of your marriage, divorce that man. It is not an easy thing to do, and nobody enjoys a divorce, but sometimes it is a decision that needs to be taken. Do it before you add another one," Mee Fennie said, pointing at little Taati whom I was breastfeeding. Now I am breastfeeding little Shopi,' Kauna said laughing and tickled her baby's chubby cheeks.

'I was determined to take Mee Fennie's advice and I promised her that I would talk to my mother. However, she warned me about how she might react.

' "Your mother will certainly not approve of you wanting to divorce your husband, because when I divorced, she was angry with me. She gave me this long lecture that marriages are not easy and what did I expect, bla, bla, bla, bla. She claimed that I embarrassed her, our parents and the rest of the clan. For a long time she did not want to be seen with me in public," Mee

Fennie told me. Nevertheless, I still thought I would try my luck. Listen to what my mother said.

'"Ntowele, how do you expect your little mother to advise you? She is divorced herself. I hate to say this, but divorced people can give no other advice. Talk to married people, people who know how to handle marriage problems, not those who ran away from them. Besides, you forget a very important thing. Shange is the man God has given you and you must accept him as he is. You have made a promise before Him and the whole congregation to love and cherish your husband till death do you part. You cannot break your word now," she told me. That was the end of the discussion. So I just gave up. I'm tired. Now, when he beats me, I simply nurse my wounds. Maybe my mother was right, this is the man God has given me and I must accept him, bad as he is.'

'Kauna, God has nothing to do with bad men and bad marriages. You must stop talking like this.'

'The truth is, I have nowhere to go,' she said. 'Mother told me that a divorce will have a really bad effect on Daddy's preaching.'

'"Your brother Blacky has done more than enough damage to his career. His crazy lifestyle and his subsequent death have affected him more than you know. Your father does not always say these things, but I know how he feels. You are strong, Kauna, and I know you will find a solution to your problem. This difficulty may sort itself out. You may be surprised. Shange may outgrow his temper and you two will be fine together again. Be patient," my mother advised me.'

◆

'Where, anyway, did you meet your husband?' I asked Kauna one day.

'I met him through my brother Blacky, whom I used to tease that he "sold me into slavery". They worked together at the mine. Whenever they came to visit, mother would not let Shange travel at night because of the curfew. He would go on to his village the next morning. Our house was like a transit hotel for him. Their visits were always exciting. They would come with the latest cars and bring us presents and money. Mother was impressed with Shange. She thought he was a very well-brought-up gentleman. Father was not so sure. He wanted us to wait. I wish I had listened. But before I knew it, I was married.

'A year or so after my wedding, Blacky died in a mysterious car accident. We never really knew what happened. There was so much speculation. He had a wound in his head which looked as if it had been made by a bullet. The dents on his car were suspicious. He was apparently last seen with his girlfriend, Tuna. She denied this. She said Blacky and a friend had dropped her at a friend's house at Ongwediva with the promise that he would pick her up later that night. She claimed that he never returned. But some say he did, and that he spent the night with her at Ongwediva. Others say he was last seen with his colleagues from the mine. Everyone, male and female, denied seeing him last. Their stories were all so contradictory. In the end, we buried my brother without really knowing what was what. Had he been killed in a car accident or had somebody killed him?

'For some reason we were not surprised at the way in which he died. Every time we had an unexpected visitor, our first thought was always that something had happened to Blacky. He lived a fast life. And you know the saying, "You die the way you live."

'My brother had money and all kinds of friends. Each time he came to see us, he had a new car, a different girlfriend and a new brand of alcohol. My parents talked, preached and pleaded with Blacky to change his lifestyle. Mee Fennie, in her usual manner, scolded him one day after he had been assaulted and robbed at the *cuca* shops and could not remember who had attacked him.

' "My son, alcohol has its owners. It is not for us. It is not for our clan. Look at what has happened to all the members of your clan who have abused alcohol. If you don't stop, it will destroy you. It is having men such as you in our clan that causes our husbands, and other men, to abuse and bully us. You think of no one but yourselves, and you are not respected."

'I also tried to make him see what an awful situation he put father in and how he was embarrassing all of us. He would cry, apologise and promise to change, but nothing ever came of his promises. I never knew what went wrong. I think it was the mine. It changed him into somebody we could no longer recognise. Initially he went to the mine with our uncle to do a holiday job when he finished high school. There was an opportunity for him to go overseas with a church scholarship. Father was working very hard on that. Blacky was very intelligent but chose the mine above his education. His crazy behaviour was hard for my parents.'

She kept quiet for a minute or so, cleared her throat and continued. 'My heart went out to my father. People started to talk about us. "*Aana yáasita*,"* they would say. Statements such as "Clean your own front doors first before you tell us to clean ours" were thrown at my parents.

'Father handled my brother's behaviour quite well. When he preached about the conduct of young people, he would always make reference to my brother.

* 'Children of pastors.'

69

' "For those who know my son Blacky . . ."

' "Young people like my son Blacky . . ."

' "They don't listen to the teaching of their parents, teachers and leaders." My father even conducted Blacky's funeral service himself. At one point, he broke down but he still continued. "Maybe it was better this way," he commented days after the funeral. My father is the strongest person I have ever seen. Mother, on the other hand, could not handle Blacky's behaviour. You would swear she was the pastor. She wanted to die of embarrassment. She didn't even want father to make any reference to my brother in his preaching.

' "You should have told me that you were going to talk about my son like that. I wouldn't have gone to church," she would complain. Blacky was her *Shiveli*, her pride and first joy. I think she favoured him above all of us,' Kauna said and smiled to herself.

'Anyways,' she took a deep breath. 'He was my darling brother and protector. He was the most handsome man I have ever seen. It was as if he'd been handcrafted to perfection. He was tall and ebony black. Grandmother nicknamed him Blacky when he was a baby. He had very thick eyebrows that almost met at the middle of his forehead. Below those eyebrows were his big brown eyes. The girls were crazy about them. His strong healthy teeth looked whiter every time he smiled. He was a tall man, with almost the figure and stature of Shange. People at the mine would ask if they were brothers.

'My handsome brother . . . Although he acted crazy at times, I loved him. He was so full of life and humour. You wouldn't ever be depressed when he was around.'

I looked at Kauna's large eyes and very dark, almost shiny complexion and could see how handsome Blacky must have been.

'You miss him?' I asked.

'Yes, I miss him. I miss him very much.' Her face was a mask of sadness.

That was the first and only occasion that she talked to me so comfortably about her late brother Blacky.

Chapter Seven

Amazingly, Shange did not touch Kauna again. My fears that all hell would break loose once she was discharged from hospital were forgotten. He did not even confront her. At first, Kauna did not trust him; she thought it was just a matter of time before her husband beat her again. But it did not happen. From that moment, Mukwankala became Kauna's goddess. Mukwankala this and Mukwankala that ... Mukwankala punctuated her every sentence. Kauna made an *onyoka* necklace of ostrich shells for her as a gesture of appreciation.

'Mukwankala, I don't know what you said or did to him, but whatever it was, it worked!' she told the old woman. 'He has stopped abusing me. He doesn't beat me any more. He has a naturally bad temper, but now he turns away from things that once he would have slapped me for. At first, I thought it was just a matter of time. I was waiting for him to attack me, but now I don't think he will ever touch me again. It's over, I can feel it,' she said, touching her heart. 'People often talked to him after he had beaten me, but it did not help at all. This time it is different. He has genuinely changed.'

'My child,' Mukwankala said, putting her hand gently on Kauna's tiny shoulders, 'we are all children of God and no child of God should be treated as you were. Even God, who created us, does not treat us like this. Why should Shange feel he has the right to abuse you, you of all people, and then claim to be a Christian? My late husband used to ask our sons – you know we only have boys,' she reminded us. ' "Do you see me beating your mother? Do you see me abusing her?" and he would tell them, "I don't want to hear of you beating your women. It is only a coward who does such a thing." It is not because he was a pastor, he was just a good man.'

Mukwankala became Kauna's confidante and counsellor. Whenever she had a problem, my friend would go to her for advice – like the occasion when she wanted to visit her parents and Shange would not let her go.

'Mukwankala, my husband doesn't want me to visit my parents,' she complained. 'I need a break. I need to go home. I miss my people.'

'Child, a husband doesn't want his wife to visit her parents if she is unhappy, especially if he has just beaten her. He thinks you will report him. Don't visit your parents as if you were running away. He can feel it and will see right through your request. If you want your husband to allow you to visit your family, behave like a happy wife. Take good care of yourself, eat well and gain some weight. Hang on for a while, let him forget about your unhappiness and the beatings and then ask him. He will not let you visit your parents in this state. You are too thin and your unhappiness is written all over your face,' she said, examining Kauna closely.

'What if I gain weight and he still doesn't let me go?'

'Believe me, he will. Just behave like a serious happy wife,' she said with that I-know-what-I-am-talking-about expression on her face.

For a person with a small appetite like Kauna, it was not easy to eat more than necessary. Sustera's help was called for. She gave her a lot of vitamins and syrup and prescribed a new 'diet'. Her treatment worked like a miracle. Kauna ate all the time. I shared some of my bean soup with her. Mukwankala sent her a delicious goat stew full of vegetables. We literally fed her as if we were feeding a mother who had

73

just had a baby. People noticed the change in her weight and appearance.

'You look good.'

'Shange is treating you well these days.'

'You have a new boyfriend?' some would tease her.

Even her husband noticed. Although he didn't say anything, his looks said it all. It was time. She took one long deep breath and approached her Shange.

'Why don't you wait for the school holiday? It is less than two weeks away. Then my niece Shiwa and Nkelo can help me with the kids,' Shange replied when Kauna asked him if she could visit her parents.

Kauna lost her voice. She hadn't expected him to give her permission just like that!

'Unless . . .'

'No, no, it's fine. It will be perfect. Yes, somebody to help with the kids. Yes, yes, you are right,' she said, struggling to find the right words.

'OK, then we wait until school break.' Shange lit a cigarette.

'Thank you, thank you very much,' she stuttered.

'It's OK. You haven't visited your people for some time now. You should visit them.' He actually smiled. Kauna thanked her husband again, left the living room quickly and went straight to her hut.

◆

My daughter and Kauna's three daughters, Kandiwapa, Lilly and Taati, accompanied Kauna and little Shopi to the main road to catch a ride to Ondangwa. The four girls each carried a piece of Kauna's luggage and walked a few metres ahead of us.

'Shange offered to drive me home,' Kauna remarked, looking at the dusty road in front ahead.

'And you declined the offer?'

'Yes . . .'

'Why, Kauna?'

'What will Shange and I say to each other on that long journey? Besides I am not used to him being so nice to me,' she said. I kept quiet.

'There is a car coming, Mommy, must we stop it?' Kandiwapa called out.

'You are lucky today,' I said to Kauna as we helped her and little Shopi climb on to an open *bakkie* belonging to one of the *cuca* shop owners. The three girls kissed their mother and their little brother goodbye. My daughter and I did likewise.

'You take care of your father and the children,' Kauna told Kandiwapa.

'Yes, Meme, I will.'

'Make sure they have all their meals and if you need anything you know where to go?'

'Yes, Meme, to Mee Ali,' she said obediently.

'Mammy,' Kandiwapa whispered in her mother's ear.

'Hmmm.'

'Don't stay away for too long.'

'No, I won't,' Kauna whispered back.

'Greetings to grandmother . . . and grandfather . . . and kuku Peetu . . . and kuku Fennie . . . and . . .,' the girls said, waving goodbye until the car disappeared from sight.

◆

At Ondangwa Kauna shopped for everybody. For her parents, siblings, nephews, nieces and for Mee Fennie and her children.

Shange had given her a lot of money. For some reason she didn't tell me about this. Nobody had ever given her so much money all at once. Not even when her brother Blacky worked at the mine. She had only wanted to take some of it, but Shange had insisted that she take all of it. He was happy, he insisted. Shopping for him was never that much fun. She knew the villagers would be jealous.

To find a lift to her parents' village, Omapandu, she and Shopi went to a store that belonged to a family who used to live there. She met with people who were also on their way to the village and others nearby. Some people she knew; others she didn't. They exchanged greetings and complimented her on her appearance. Kauna looked rich – all those groceries! From Ondangwa to Omapandu, Kauna and Shopi took a lift with a teacher who came to buy supplies for his *cuca* shop. They sat at the back of a Toyota *bakkie* with some others. Kauna listened to the latest gossip in what used to be her village. Who had died, who had married, who was still not pregnant after so many years of marriage, who is now too old to get married, who has moved, who has this new disease, who, who, who . . .

Kauna arrived at her parents' home late in the afternoon. Everyone was happy to see her. They immediately remarked how good she looked, better than she had done on previous occasions. For the first time in three years Kauna did not need to worry about cooking for and feeding her family. Her two younger sisters cooked her favourite dishes and would not let her fetch water or wood. They braided her hair. Even little Shopi was spoiled. They bathed him and carried him about with them. Her sisters were glued to Kauna. They wanted to know everything about her life at Oshaantu. They wanted to get married too and have plenty of children, but Kauna quickly said they should wait. They should study hard, finish school, get a career and then get married. They told her the latest news.

They gossiped about their relatives, especially their mother – that she hadn't changed a bit and still worried about what other people said about her family. They told her that kuku Peetu still didn't have a wife, even though his hair was now turning grey. They laughed a lot. Kauna was home!

'What did you do to get that scar?' her mother asked.

He caught me in bed with another man, Kauna felt like saying, but decided against it. She was not sure what to tell her mother.

Kauna visited her parents for a week and then went to spend another week at Mee Fennie's. She looked forward to seeing her aunt, whom she hadn't seen for more than three years.

Mee Fennie and her children recognised Kauna from a distance of about two hundred metres. They all went out to welcome her.

'OMee Kauna,' they cried out.

'*Ongaame*,' she responded to their cheerful welcoming.

'OMee Kauna . . .'

'*Ongaame* . . .'

'*Oye naanaa* . . .'

They literally lifted Kauna and her baby off the ground and she almost lost her balance. She was glad that Shange had suggested that she visit her people during the school vacation. It gave her the opportunity to see Mee Fennie's children, who would otherwise have been at boarding school. They led her to a large open hut and helped her remove the luggage from her head. She took her baby off her back and introduced him.

'This is little Shopi. He was named after Tate Shoopala, the local pastor at our village.' The little boy was confused by the sight of so many strangers and threatened to cry. His mother reassured him that he was OK, quite quite OK.

'This place is a long way away,' Kauna remarked as she sat on the ground.

'Yes, it is far,' said one of the children.

'You kids have grown up since the last time I saw you.' The children giggled shyly.

'What grade are you in now, Kapandu?' Kauna asked Mee Fennie's eldest daughter.

'Grade eleven,' she answered, twisting her braids.

'That is good.' Kauna was genuinely impressed.

'And you, Rebecca?' Kauna asked the second daughter.

'Grade nine.'

'That's good! What about you?' Kauna asked Mee Fennie's last offspring and only son, Osha.

'Grade five,' he said proudly.

'He is the man of the house,' Mee Fennie said and gently rubbed his head with her right palm.

There had been some changes to the homestead since Kauna's first visit. Then there had only been three huts, a kitchen and two bedrooms. Now, all of the children had their own huts, and Mee Fennie had built herself a concrete bedroom. Her livestock had also increased from two goats to seven, and from two cows to five. More purple and white violets had grown around the homestead. 'You must be proud of yourself,' Kauna remarked to Mee Fennie.

'I am,' she said.

Kauna could hide her unhappy marriage behind her newly plump body but she could not hide the scar.

'The scar on your lip?' Mee Fennie frowned suspiciously.

'The scar on my lip?' Kauna repeated, touching the scar, which had become hard, with her middle finger.

'Yes, that scar!'

'Oh, the scar.' Kauna hesitated a minute and then she told Mee Fennie about the last thrashing she had had, adding quickly that the beatings had ceased.

'Everybody is surprised,' she continued. 'At first I didn't

believe it myself, but it's the truth, he doesn't beat me any more.' She was laughing in an effort to appear confident. 'He has stopped, really. He even offered to bring me home. It's just that I refused. He also gave me a lot of money.' Kauna was nervously twisting her hands. Mee Fennie did not say anything. She looked at Shopi, whom Kauna was breastfeeding.

'He is the last one. Sustera gave me something. Shange doesn't know. He would kill us both, she warned me. She is a good person . . .'

'Bring him here,' Mee Fennie said and reached out to Shopi, who was dozing. She cuddled him till he fell asleep. Kauna felt uncomfortable because Mee Fennie had not commented on what she had told her.

Three years previously when she had visited Mee Fennie, Kauna had not had any visible scars, but her thin body and bony face had betrayed the unhappiness of her marriage. Now, she expected Mee Fennie to give her another lecture about divorcing Shange. Instead the older woman kept her own counsel and simply observed Kauna. Mee Fennie did not even say a word about her 'useless' relatives. She usually had something to say about her brothers. Uncle Peetu usually got the worst of it, as Kauna recalled from her last visit.

'A drunk, that is all he is good for. No wonder his wife and children left him. He is so useless. Doesn't have a wife, never married, doesn't have a girlfriend. I don't know what is wrong with him. Your mother and I tried to fix him up with good girls, nothing. He runs so fast as if they were going to brand him. What a waste of manhood,' Mee Fennie complained.

'Your big uncle,' she said about their older brother, Joshua, 'no difference. He married a woman who beats him up, but when he comes to my house he plays the strict uncle. He preaches to *my* children that he won't tolerate any failures or misbehaviour at school and especially *no* pregnancies. "I don't want people to say that because there is no man in this house, there is disorder," he warned them. I just look at him. He, a man who cannot control his own wife and children, wants to discipline mine.' Mee Fennie was exasperated at the very thought of her brother.

'I love my uncles, they are wonderful people. Especially kuku Peetu, he is a nice person. Hardworking, and so kind, and has never caused anybody trouble,' Kauna responded.

'Hardworking, nice, kind, but that is not enough. They need to march down to your husband and give him a beating that he will remember as long as he lives,' she said. 'This is why husbands abuse us and people don't respect our clan. It is all due to men like your uncles. We don't have strong men,' she said, as if 'strong men' – whatever that meant – could perform magic.

'Strong men, like the Shallis, Kapendas, Amweeles, Uugwangas . . . nobody messes with those women – their husbands or any men from the villages – because they have strong men. Not drunks and loafers. A man is supposed to be the backbone and pillar of his clan, but look at what we have. Can you imagine, we – the women – have to take care of them as if they were disabled people,' she said, shaking her head.

'You should have been a man, Mee Fennie,' Kauna said.

'I wouldn't have minded,' she said.

◆

'How is your friend Mee Ali doing?' Mee Fennie asked Kauna, remembering me from Kauna's last visit.

'She is doing fine. She is always doing fine. She has a good husband.'

Mee Fennie and her children slaughtered a goat for Kauna

80

and prepared a large dinner to welcome her. Kauna was thrilled.

'Oh, thank you, Mother, but a goat? That is too much.'

'We only see you once in a while, so why not slaughter a goat in your honour, when that special visit happens,' her small mother replied.

Kauna, Mee Fennie and her family sat around the fire and enjoyed their dinner, chatting till past midnight.

◆

'Let us pray,' Mee Fennie said, waking Kauna up.

'Hmmm,' Kauna said through her sleep.

'Let us pray, dear,' she repeated. Kauna opened her eyes and lifted her head. It was dark in the room. She blinked a couple of times. In the dark, she could see Mee Fennie sitting with her hands folded in her lap.

'I am awake,' Kauna said and closed her eyes. The cocks have not crowed yet and Mee Fennie is awake already! Kauna thought.

Mee Fennie prayed. She thanked God for watching over her and her family; for providing for her and her children; and she asked God to guide them all. She thanked God for bringing Kauna and little Shopi safely to her house . . . Kauna woke up. 'Amen,' Mee Fennie concluded her prayer.

'Amen,' Kauna echoed. Mee Fennie got off the bed and left the hut. Kauna heard Mee Fennie exchanging greetings with her children. Kauna fell asleep again.

'I am going to the market. I will be back before sunset.' Mee Fennie's voice woke Kauna up again. She stared at the friendly face of her little mother. There was more light in the room now. The sun was slowly rising. Kauna could hear the sound of the girls pounding.

'Oh, Mother, why didn't you wake me up properly before?' Kauna asked, looking at all the food, pots, plates and cutlery in baskets and buckets.

'It is all right. I didn't want to wake you. You are tired. The girls will bring you *ontaku*.'

'I am coming with you, Mother. Let me quickly wash my face.'

'You don't have to . . .'

'No, Mother, I want to come. Besides what will I do here all day?' she said, heading for the bathroom. The girls brought her *ontaku*. Kauna drank two full *oompambas* and was about to put little Shopi on her back when Mee Fennie protested.

'Oh no, no, the baby must stay here – with the girls. They will take good care of him. The market is not a good place for babies,' she said. Kauna was a little disappointed but thought that her little mother knew best.

Kauna looked at all the food prepared for the customers and wondered how Mee Fennie was going to carry such a variety. There were two large black pots, one yellow medium-sized basin and two red buckets. In one pot, she had put baked *vetkoekies*. In the other, she had put boiled meat cut into dozens of pieces. In one red bucket there were large pieces of raw meat, and in the other, spices, salt, plastic bags and dish cloths.

'Let me help you carry some of these, Mother.' Kauna lifted the pot with *vetkoekies* in it and balanced it on her head, and she picked up the bucket containing salt and spices. Mee Fennie picked up the rest.

They followed a crawling pathway that grew so narrow at times that Kauna would stagger a little. Mee Fennie moved with such swift steps that it seemed as if she carried feathers on her head. It was a long walk to the market and Kauna was not quite ready for it.

'Maybe we should have taken a lift. What do you think?' Mee Fennie asked.

'I'm OK. How far is it again?' Kauna asked, already tired.

'It is not so far away, just behind those fig trees,' Mee Fennie said, pointing the way ahead of them. Kauna couldn't see any fig trees nearby. She sighed lightly.

The market place, commonly known as 'Omatala', was a large area situated very close to the tarred road. It was rush hour: buses, taxis and cars were speeding past, transporting people to work. Mee Fennie and Kauna literally had to run to cross the street. Cars were driven as if they owned the roads. There were dozens of stalls at the market with goods everywhere. Men and women were selling all kinds of items: second-hand clothes that were spread on plastic bags on the ground or hanging on poles; livestock, vegetables, fruit, *vetkoekies*, raw meat, roasted meat and chicken; home-brewed alcohol, *kafau*, *okatokele*, *omalovu* and the popular *tombo*. The air was filled with the aroma of fire and food. Certain smells were bearable; others made Kauna feel ill. Rubbish lay all over the place: dirty papers, empty cool-drink cans, half-eaten pieces of meat and bones.

Some people brought their livestock to be slaughtered at the market. The place where this was done was not something any customer should see. Cow and goat dung lay everywhere. Pigs sniffed round hungrily in the mud. Water from blocked drains flooded through the street.

Mee Fennie's stall stood towards the last rows of the market. Mee Fennie exchanged greetings with other vendors around her. She introduced Kauna to her neighbours: Mevrou Kepwita, Mee Doora, Benny and Tate Kamati. It was clear that the five enjoyed a good relationship.

'This is my daughter,' Mee Fennie introduced Kauna proudly.

'I come after her mother.' Kauna returned the greetings of Mee Fennie's friends.

'We thought you were not coming today,' Mee Doora said to Mee Fennie.

'You are late every morning but everybody knows you'll show up,' Mevrou Kepwita snapped at Mee Doora. Mee Doora gave Mevrou a severe look.

'I was just a little late this morning.' Mee Fennie turned to Kauna. 'Here, child, you sit on this.' She offered Kauna an empty twenty-five-litre cooking-oil container to sit on. She placed some torn pieces of cardboard on the surface to act as a cushion. Mee Fennie sat on a tree stump and started to prepare her pots, her fire and her food. She clumped wood together, then she added pieces of paper, lit them and blew some air into the fire before it burnt fiercely. Then she added salt and a mixture of spices – some of which she had mixed herself – to the various dishes she had made.

Kauna studied Mee Fennie's neighbours. Mevrou Kepwita's stall caught her attention. It was quite fancy. It almost looked like a small shop and appeared huge when compared to other stalls. A tent provided her goods with shade. She had a beautiful armchair to sit in that she had brought from home. A long plank resting on two drums served as a counter. She didn't sell meat or alcohol like her neighbours but *vetkoekies*, sweets, cheap jewellery, handbags, biscuits and lipsticks. Her appearance was another wonder. She wore an Afro wig that was shiny and greasy, eye-shadow and what Kauna thought was some kind of powder on her face – later Mee Fennie told her it was egg yellow, an ingredient used for baking cakes. She wore elaborate beads around her neck and gold and silver bracelets. She had a radio, which she would only turn on for the news. She stood by her stall wearing her big sunglasses as if she did not belong there. Kauna thought Mevrou was too dressed up for the market.

Tate Kamati's stall was made of thick strong planks also resting on two drums. He sold meat, slices of bread and *tombo*. He chopped the meat as fast as if he were in a butchery. He was a master at mixing various spices to create the best one, which he only shared with his immediate neighbours. He cooked some meat in a huge pot, but most of it he roasted on hot charcoals. He was large and tall. He seemed like a man of very few words. How he fitted into the company of Mee Fennie and her friends was a riddle.

Then there was Benny, a young man who was about twenty-five years old. He sold meat, sweets and soft drinks. He had a friendly face and an easy smile.

Finally, there was Mee Doora, who sold meat, *vetkoekies* and *tombo*. She was short, fat and loud. Her laughter was terrible: she laughed as if she had a hacking cough. Her shoulders and big stomach jiggled when she laughed. Kauna imagined that her mother would call such a woman 'No lady'. Mee Doora had dark incision marks just below her cheekbones and above her eyebrows, in sharp contrast to her light complexion. Her big eyes looked as if they would fall out every time she moved them. She had long braids tied in a pony-tail style behind her head that made her face look rounder. As usual she had something to tell her neighbours. Today her news was of a man who, apparently, put 'things' in his *tombo* to make people buy more of it.

'Did you people hear what happened last night, at Okapale village, at Mashaka's shebeen?' she asked, looking at everyone's face. 'Did you hear they found a penis in his *tombo*?'

'Found what?' Benny asked, shocked and amused at the same time.

'You heard me, Bennytjie, you heard me,' Mee Doora said, nodding, satisfied by Benny's shocked reaction. She continued, 'The penis was taken to the hospital and the doctors confirmed that indeed it was a penis-penis. A man's penis. So when the customers found out, they were of course furious and beat Mashaka to death. Now everybody is saying, "Those who drunk Mashaka's *tombo* also took a sip from somebody's penis."' Mee Doora acted disgusted. She was amused by her own story, resting her hands on her knees, lifting her feet and striking them repeatedly on the ground: as she laughed, dimples formed on both her plump cheeks. Mashaka's popular shebeen was about ten kilometres east of the gravel road to the market. Suddenly Mee Doora turned to Benny.

'Hey, Bennytjie, that is your village, you're from Okapale too, aren't you? Haven't you drunk *tombo* from Mashaka's shebeen?' Mee Doora asked, feigning uncertainty. Before Benny could respond, Tate Kamati interrupted sharply.

'What kind of a woman are you? Talking about private parts in public just like that. You laugh so loudly all your teeth show. You fart in public and drink like a man. Sometimes I wonder how you ever got a husband.' His outburst surprised everybody, except Benny. He laughed until he nearly cried. Mee Doora gave Benny a severe look and the laughter from his face disappeared instantly. Benny looked at Tate Kamati and coughed a couple of times to dampen another burst of laughter which was threatening to explode. Mee Doora turned to Tate Kamati.

'And what is wrong with you, Kamati? I was not even talking to you, or did you drink from Mashaka's *tombo* by any chance?' Silence.

'Does Tate Kamati look like somebody who drinks *tombo* from that kind of a place?' Mevrou asked.

'Yes, does he look like that to you?' Mee Fennie supported Mevrou's question.

'People, now, why are you all attacking me? All I was doing,' she shrugged her shoulders innocently, 'was telling you what happened at this one's village,' Mee Doora said, pointing again at Benny. She turned to Tate Kamati.

'Eh-he, you want to tell me your wife doesn't fart?' Mee Doora asked, putting her arms akimbo and pushing her head forward like somebody who was challenging him to a fight.

'The other day I heard over the radio that the Minister has said they will sell this place to one person. And this person will charge us all a lot of money individually and per day, if we don't keep this place clean and use water wisely,' Mevrou said, changing the subject.

'Well, if people don't want to keep the market clean and keep wasting water, the government should sell it,' replied Mee Fennie.

Mee Doora decided to visit other stalls. She asked Mee Fennie to watch her stall. She walked with her hands on her hips as if the whole market place belonged to her.

'She spends more time gossiping, and bothering people at their stalls, than selling her goods,' Mevrou said, talking more to herself than to anybody else. Kauna watched everything with a keen interest.

'We miss her when she does not come,' Mee Fennie whispered to Kauna.

'I can imagine,' Kauna said, smiling.

'Here, child.' Mee Fennie gave Kauna a plate with a piece of meat and two *vetkoekies* topped with sauce. Kauna was not hungry, but took the food and ate it anyway.

'Thank you, Mother,' she said.

'Here, here, Benny, eh . . . give my daughter a tin of Fanta,'

87

Mee Fennie called on Benny. 'I am buying from you now, so you will buy your lunch from me.'

'It's OK, Mee Fennie, keep the money. Let me pay for her, to welcome her,' he responded in a friendly way.

'Oh, thank you, Benny, it is very thoughtful of you. I will definitely slaughter a cow for you when you get married.' Everyone laughed.

'Benny has a fancy hair cut,' Kauna remarked.

'My daughter says, you have a fancy hair cut.'

'Mother!' Kauna called out, embarrassed.

'Oh, thank you, Meme . . . ?'

'Mee Kauna,' Mee Fennie helped Benny out.

'Mee Kauna,' he said, apologetically. 'It is a Mike Tyson haircut. The girls are crazy about this style.' He patted his head with a big smile.

'Please watch my stall, I am going to the bathroom,' Mevrou asked Mee Fennie.

'*Eewa*, Mevrou,' Mee Fennie agreed. Mevrou turned to Kauna and said she could sit under the shade of her tent if she would like to.

'The heat can be unbearable here.'

'Thank you, Mee Kepwi . . .' Mee Fennie poked Kauna on the side. 'Mevrou,' Kauna said louder. 'Thank you, Mevrou, thank you so much,' she thanked her again. Mevrou smiled and left.

'Why is she called "Mevrou"?' Kauna asked Mee Fennie as soon as she had gone.

'She was a teacher for almost twenty years and then she was dismissed from her work because she did not have certain papers from a higher class. She is quite bitter with the government,' Mee Fennie answered.

' "To think our own government could do this to me! I feel stabbed in the back. I taught them how to read and write. I taught them how to clean their snotty noses and clean their behinds and now after independence, I am not good enough! To be treated like this by my own people! And that big-eared Minister, I held his hand when he wrote his first letter down. I applauded him when he beamed with pride. It was me who told him that he could do it. It was me who did this and did that." She complains endlessly in this way.

'She insists on being called "Mevrou". Please call her this, we all do,' Mee Fennie warned Kauna.

'OK,' Kauna said, not entirely sure that she understood why.

Kauna was fascinated by the manner in which the vendors conducted their business. Every time any prospective customers passed by, they competed for them. They would offer them discounts and presents if they came to buy from their stall.

'Sister, brother, come buy here.'

'Buy here. I will give you this for half the price.'

'It is fresh and delicious.'

'This has the best spice.'

'All these intestines are yours for free if you buy here.'

It was astonishing how they competed for customers and still maintained a good relationship with each other.

Some vendors made special efforts to attract visitors. They kept their stalls clean, had cutlery, warm water and towels for their customers to use, some even had a chair or two. Others did not seem to care about the look of their food or their own appearance. Nevertheless, business at the market seemed to go well. The home-brew business was hard to compete with. Wherever Kauna looked, men and women held a glass of the popular *tombo*.

'We miss the students,' Mee Fennie said, looking at her watch. 'This is about their tea break. They are our biggest customers. Usually all these *vetkoekies* and *tombo* would be into a third round by now.'

'*Tombo*, they drink *tombo*?' Kauna asked, surprised.

'Oh yes, wearing their school uniform. We feel sorry for those teachers,' Mee Fennie said, amused. 'When schools close for vacation, we don't do as much business. We normally can't wait for the schools to reopen,' she said with a smile.

Mee Fennie noticed a young man wearing oversized jeans and a white T-shirt with '*I was in New York*' written in red letters. He wore dark glasses so that his eyes couldn't be seen. He walked from stall to stall buying nothing. He would ask for the price of items, but showed more interest in the women's purses. He came towards Mee Fennie's stall and asked to buy a piece of meat.

'It is all finished, son,' Mee Fennie said quickly.

'Mother, you still have plenty,' Kauna innocently reminded Mee Fennie.

'It is all gone, Kauna.'

'But you just cooked and you still had . . .'

'Kauna, the few pieces left are our dinner.' She gave Kauna a severe look. The young woman got the message.

'Oh yes, Mother, how could I have forgotten? I am sorry, my brother, I forgot. Yes, the meat is all finished,' Kauna mumbled, avoiding his stare. The young man smiled, left them and disappeared into the tea crowd. His expensive sports shoes left tracks that Kauna felt like wiping away.

'He wanted to rob you?' Kauna asked, shocked.

'Child, keep your eyes open. This is not Oshaantu. Welcome to the *omatalas*.'

'I don't think I could live in a town,' Kauna said, watching the people with a new interest. Mee Fennie noticed the concerned look on her face.

'Are you OK, Kauna?'

'Yes, Mother, I'm fine. Why do people drive so recklessly?'

'I don't know, child. Children and old people get hit and killed all the time here.'

At lunchtime the government officials came to the market to buy their food. They were Mee Fennie, Mevrou, Mee Doora, Tate Kamati and Benny's best customers. Some were Mevrou's former grade one pupils. They went straight to her stall. Again Kauna was introduced. 'She is my daughter. I follow her mother,' Mee Fennie said proudly. She knew the favourite dishes of some of her customers.

'Your kidneys, liver and intestines are here, cooked just as you like,' she said. The men had tremendous appetites. Kauna watched them as they dipped the *vetkoekies* layered with pieces of meat into the gravy and pushed them into their mouths. As they ate, they updated Mee Fennie and Mevrou on the latest government issues. When they had finished their lunch, Mee Fennie provided them with warm water and a clean cloth. Kauna helped with the dishes.

'End of the month they tip me big,' Mee Fennie said with a smile as she dried the dishes. 'Do you know why the government workers buy from us?' she asked. Kauna shook her head. 'We keep ourselves and our place clean and we also cook well,' Mee Fennie complimented herself.

'What do other vendors think of your popularity with all these customers?'

'Some of them say we use *muti* to attract them.'

At midday, the heat intensified as did the flies that were buzzing all over the place. Vendors used pieces of cardboard to frighten them away; some only did so when they saw customers approaching. Kauna sat there observing the commotion of vendors, customers and passing vehicles. A baby crawling in the dirt reminded her of little Shopi and she felt the milk swelling in her breasts. This is really no place for babies, she thought. She noticed the young man with his oversized jeans and his '*I was in New York*' T-shirt again. He walked towards them. He stopped at Benny's stall and asked for sweets. With his dark glasses hanging over his nose he watched Kauna. She tried to attract Mee Fennie's attention, but the woman was busy with a customer. His gaze was fixed on Kauna. She felt uncomfortable. Then the young man moved very fast. He snatched money from a woman who was about to pay for a piece of roasted meat from Tate Kamati. The young man ran, pushing people to the side. Tate Kamati grabbed his panga from under his counter and chased the thief. Despite his huge body, he moved fast. The women and children screamed. As the young man ran across the street, Tate Kamati threw the panga. Kauna held her breath. The women put their hands on their heads, screaming. Everyone watched as the panga flew across the street, missed a man on a bicycle and a passing teenager, and with amazing accuracy hit the young man in his back. The thief screamed as if he had been branded. He staggered down the tarred road and fell, bringing traffic to a standstill. Tate Kamati walked up to the bleeding man, and with a look of contempt, picked up his panga and his money and left him lying in the street. People surrounded the wounded man. 'Memeee,' he groaned with pain.

'Please, somebody take him to the hospital,' a person in the crowd called out.

'He was stealing,' others protested.

'Here, here,' one of the onlookers waved at a police van. Two police officers jumped out of the van and started to shout wildly.

'Who did this? Who did this?' demanded one. People looked at the police officer as if he were speaking a new language.

'Who did this?' The thief on the ground groaned louder still.

'We are asking you people,' the other police officer asked threateningly.

'Help me please, help me,' the thief cried.

'This man will die here while you are asking questions. Why don't you take him to the hospital first and then come back later for your questions?' Mevrou bravely told the officers.

'Yes,' the crowd agreed with her. Some men helped to put the thief into the back of the van and the police left with him. The vendors, remembering their goods, hurried back to their stalls.

An hour later the police van returned with a third police officer. The third police officer, who was carrying a loud-speaker, started to address the vendors and customers.

'Please, people, we want to remind you again. Don't take the law into your own hands. Report any incidents of theft to your nearest police station.'

The vendors went about their business as if the police announcement were unimportant. A while later Mevrou's husband arrived with a yellow Volkswagen combi to pick her up. He smiled and greeted the vendors as he passed them by. Again Kauna was introduced. He asked her about her village and both were pleasantly surprised that he knew some of her people. During the day he transported people between Oshakati and Ondangwa. If he happened to be in this area, he came by for lunch, but he had not been today, he told Kauna. He dismantled the tent neatly and loaded everything into the Volkswagen. The stall took up all the space in the combi. Mevrou, only carrying her handbag and small basket, bid goodbye to her neighbours.

'She always looks as if she is moving home,' Mee Doora said to Kauna. Mee Fennie gave her a severe look.

One by one, the vendors started to pack up their goods. As they said goodbye to one another it felt like one big family. It had been quite a day. Apart from the incident with the thief, Kauna had enjoyed herself.

'Benny seems a nice young man,' Kauna remarked to Mee Fennie on their way home.

'Oh yes,' she agreed. 'He is a fine young man. Other people his age go around doing all kinds of mischievous deeds, but Benny is an honest man. He will go far in life. We bless him all the time,' she said fondly.

◆

Kauna's visit to Mee Fennie was like a holiday. She enjoyed the time she spent with her little mother and her children. Although Mee Fennie did not give Kauna one of those 'divorce Shange' lectures, her non-verbal message was loud and clear. It was up to Kauna to decide what to do!

On her way home, Kauna stopped by to see her parents again. Her mother was curious to know how her visit had gone.

'So what is your small mother saying this time?'

'She sends her greetings to you all.'

Kauna's mother was very suspicious when her daughter did not give her any more information, but at the same time could not bring herself to ask whether Mee Fennie had again advised her to divorce Shange.

'You look better. It seems as if Mee Fennie took good care of you,' her mother remarked on her daughter's vibrant appearance.

Returning to Oshaantu was not as frightening this time as it had been on previous occasions. Kauna missed her children and was looking forward to seeing me again. She was a little sad to say goodbye to her relatives and old friends. Her weight had deceived many people.

'You look much much better this time.'

'We hear he has changed.'

'We hear he is not treating you well, but look at you.'

We hear, we hear, we hear! Where do they hear whatever they hear? Kauna thought, irritated.

Kauna's father said he would accompany her to the main road to wait for a lift.

'Child,' he said, 'don't wait until it is too late. I know your mother wants your marriage to work. But I have seen women who have died in this thing called marriage, or have done things you don't want to hear about. I don't want it to get to this. Don't think of me, or my work. You must do what you think is best for you.'

Chapter Eight

One afternoon Kauna and I were having one of our quiet conversations when a young man, a cousin of Shange's, came towards the hut. He greeted us politely and informed Kauna that the great uncle Sheya wanted to see her.

'The great uncle who?' Kauna asked, not seeming to remember the name.

'The great uncle Sheya,' he said, sounding genuinely surprised that Kauna did not seem to know whom he was talking about. 'The great uncle Sheya from Omuthiya village.'

'From Omuthiya village?'

'Yes, the very one. He wants to see you. You must come with me now,' he said.

'Come with you . . . Now? . . . Where?'

'*Koshinyanga.*'

'I . . . I don't know.'

'Maybe you should go,' I whispered to Kauna. *Oshinyanga* is the place where men meet to discuss important matters. It was only a minute away from the homestead and if the men had gathered there, the meeting was important.

'OK, wait for me outside. I am coming now.'

I found it somewhat strange . . . in fact disrespectful that the great uncle Sheya, whoever he was, would call Kauna out of her hut. I would expect him – or anyone else who needed to talk to her – to come to the hut. On the other hand, had she not gone, she risked causing real offence. Left alone, I decided to go and see if everything was all right with my mother-in-law and my children. I was just about to leave for home when the young man returned.

'Are you looking for me?' I asked him.

'Yes, Mee Ali. Kuku Sheya said I should call you as well,' he said. My heart went boom!

'Why? What is happening? Is something wrong? Why should I be there? Is Kauna OK?' I asked the young man a host of questions as I followed him through the many hallways of the homestead. He did not answer me immediately.

'They are asking her questions.'

'What questions?'

'There they are. This is where you should go,' he said, pointing at a group of people sitting under the *oshinyanga*, a large open hut. The young man disappeared, leaving me with no further directions. Hesitantly, I joined the group. There was silence while everybody waited for me to make myself comfortable on the ground.

'Mee Ali . . .,' Simoni, one of Shange's relatives, said. He appeared to be chairing the meeting. 'We were waiting for Kuku Sheya to arrive before we called this meeting,' he went on, pointing at an elderly man with a long white beard sitting on a brownish cow skin. 'He farms very far away at Omuthiya village and as you know it is not easy to get transport from that area.' He cracked the joints of his fingers one by one. It irritated me. I looked around. They were all there – Shange's mother, his sisters, brothers, small mothers, uncles, cousins, nephews, nieces and some other distant relatives – looking like vultures greedily waiting to attack their prey. There were familiar faces, which I had seen before, and others that I had never seen. Kauna sat among them, a long way away from me. We exchanged looks. She did not seem surprised that the Shanges had planned this meeting behind her back.

I looked around again. I was surprised to notice the presence of Tate Thomasa and his wife Lucia. Kauna told me that they had once had a terrible quarrel with Shange, Apparently, Thomasa in his rage had shouted at Shange, 'I will not talk to you ever again and don't ever talk to me again. If I die, don't bury me and if you die, I will not bury you.' Death had changed all that, I guess.

The slender man who had previously been introduced to kuku Sheya spoke. 'As relatives of the deceased, we want to know how somebody who was not sick and did not complain of any illness died just like that, just like an animal.' He turned to Kauna.

'Child, we only want you to tell us exactly what happened. You and your children were the last people to see Shange alive,' he said, still smoking his pipe. The whole place stank of tobacco. Kauna told her story, very briefly.

'What do you mean? He came home, sat down and died? What kind of an explanation is that? Remember we are talking about Shange here, a human being, not a cow! Tell us something else,' kuku Sheya yelled.

'I told you, he did not sleep at home, he . . .'

'We don't need to hear that. You have told the whole village that already. The point is that he was alive when he came home,' kuku Sheya interrupted her sharply. 'Even animals get sick,' he said. 'Yes, even animals get sick. They don't just drop dead like that.'

Shange's niece, Shiwa, started to cry loudly. I wondered what such a display of sorrow was about. They were not even close. We had to wait a while for her to stop and calm down.

I couldn't stand it any more. I felt I just couldn't sit there and watch them tear her apart. I decided to say something. I chose my words carefully.

'I am sure the doctors and nurses at the hospital can help us find the cause of Shange's death. These days people can look healthy and strong and then suddenly . . .,' I said, looking at the crowd, 'they just die. We can't see some of the life-threatening diseases that people carry around – diseases of the heart and high blood pressure,' I continued, trying to use the information that Sustera had shared with us on Monday. 'I don't think Kauna can provide us with an answer now. We will not know exactly what caused his death until a post mortem is done on his body. For now I think we should wait,' I concluded. They looked at me as if I had another head, that of a cow perhaps. Did I look foolish?

'Kauna was the last person who saw Shange alive and she was the last person who gave him food, which she claims he did not eat,' kuku Sheya shouted in my ears. I felt helpless.

Shiwa, who had now stopped crying, asked, 'By the way, tell us how you can be a witness if, as Mee Kauna said, you only came on the scene after my uncle had died?'

'Well, Mee Maita and I saw him arriving the morning he . . .'

'Unless you know what killed him,' a woman whose face I'd never seen before interrupted me.

What are you insinuating? You witch, I thought, upset.

'Kauna, you are a good child. You are well brought up. Shange was not a perfect man. He made mistakes like any other human being. Maybe he did things to you that we don't know about, and you got angry . . .' I thought Kauna's eyes would fall out! 'We are not accusing you of anything. But it is important for us to know the truth about what killed our Shange. That is all. You don't have to answer today, but we need to know.' Simoni concluded the first phase of the meeting. I looked at the married women and thought, are you not afraid that a similar thing might happen to you, if your husband died? How would you feel if your in-laws treated you like this?

'While we are all here, we would also like to know about the wealth of our relative.' Another man took over from kuku

Sheya and Simoni. 'We need to know about his money, bank accounts, insurance policies, his cattle and all sorts of other things. Who owes him what and whom does he owe and so on.'

How could she know? I thought. It was unlikely that Shange ever gave Kauna information about his personal financial matters.

'Do you honestly think I would know anything about Shange's wealth?' Kauna asked, looking at them all. I saw that she was shocked. How could they imagine that Shange would ever give Kauna his money for safekeeping? If I had been nearer, I would have kicked her. Why did she even bother to respond?

'Some of us here have wives and we are familiar with the expression, "a woman is the house". Wives are the people closest to their husbands. It is only the wife who knows where her husband keeps his wealth. Where is Shange's wealth? None of us here knows where it is,' he said, shrugging his shoulders.

'Most, if not all, of you, were aware of our marriage situation. You knew how he treated me. Do you honestly think that he would entrust me with his money and the papers you are talking about?' Kauna asked bravely. Silence fell.

'If you, his wife, claim to know nothing about your own husband's wealth, who will know? We the uncles don't know, his sisters and brothers don't know, his nieces and nephews don't know, even his own mother doesn't know . . .'

'Ask the woman from the white house. She may know,' Kauna said as if she didn't care any longer what might befall her.

'Ask the woman from where?' Shange's relatives responded with one voice.

'That woman, the one for whom he built a tin house.' Silence fell again. Somewhere behind us, we all heard the sound of a child crying and his mother comforting him. Another woman was looking for Mee Sofia. 'Has anybody here seen Mee Sofia?'

'Listen here, Kauna, this is very serious . . .'

'I don't know if he owes anybody money or if there is anybody out there who owes him money or anything else. All the cattle are his except for a few goats and pigs. That is all I know. As for the rest, I don't know,' Kauna responded. I pulled the edge of my skirt to my eyes and dried the tears that were threatening to fall down my face.

'Listen here, Kauna, daughter of Nambili,' kuku Sheya yelled all of a sudden, sending a tremor of fear through my body. 'You women these days go about making business out of your dead husbands' inheritance and this must come to an end. Your husbands' bodies are still cold and you are already sleeping around. Such things are not tolerated in our clan. We are not going to allow this. Never! Shange has brothers and sisters, and his mother is still alive and he is her son. She is the one who gave birth to him and brought him up. So don't you forget that! You cannot come from nowhere and think you can grab everything from her, just like that. Everything must come to the table and should be shared equally among family members. We want to do this peacefully and we need your co-operation.'

When kuku Sheya had stopped shouting, there were nods of agreement from all Shange's relatives, and for a good hour they all took turns to say the same thing in different words.

Kauna sat silently, almost indifferently, while the anger raged about her.

At one point she repeated, 'There is nothing I can do. I know nothing. You can get angry and shout at me, but it will do no good. I know nothing and I can't make things up.' But this only served to infuriate them even more.

I felt increasingly helpless and miserable. I wished Michael was with us. Had this been so, I didn't think they would have dared to be so rude and so cruel. I did not know who was worse, the men or the women. Greed demonstrated itself equally among them. The question whether Shange owed anybody anything was never raised, forgotten I guess.

Eventually they fell silent. And feeling as if we'd been beaten, we made our silent way home like two naughty children after a disciplinary hearing.

'Kauna, I don't think you should have reminded them of how you were treated in your marriage. They know. Don't push them too far, it will make matters worse for you.'

'Ali, it doesn't matter how I behave or what I say, what will be done will be done,' she said, making herself comfortable on the bed in her hut, but which now felt like our hut. She stared at the thatched roof, her arms by her sides. I pulled the trunk of the tree closer to the bed and sat down. I stroked her right arm gently.

◆

The whole confrontation reminded me of the funeral of Michael's cousin, Victor. I still vividly remember how they tore that poor widow apart. I thought that because they lived in a town, Victor's relatives would be embarrassed to be so greedy. But what I saw at that mourning house had scared me. The way they treated Victor's widow, Mee Sara, was inhumane.

Victor, who also worked at the mine, had got sick and could no longer work. Mee Sara took her husband to all the hospitals you could think of. Each time she was told that there was nothing that the doctors could do for her husband. He should go home and wait because he had an incurable disease. Victor's disease was strange. Nobody had seen anything like it. He had blisters all over his body. First, they thought it was a disease of the water. Then the blisters disappeared and sores came instead.

He had non-stop diarrhoea. He lost more than half his weight, even though there was plenty of food in his house. His wife took him to various herbalists. They did not help him. In the end he was like a baby, he did everything in his pants. Mee Sara nursed him throughout his illness. She watched her husband fading away and finally dying.

When Victor died, his relatives went to see the Great *Ngaanga* from the River, well known as the 'all-wise' and 'all-knowing', to find out who had bewitched Victor. The Great *Ngaanga* applied a mixture of mud, red clay and oil all over his face, arms and chest. He wore animal skins and burnt incense. He closed his eyes and inhaled the smoke as if it were the best smell he had ever inhaled in his life. Suddenly he opened his eyes, 'IT WAS THE WIFE! MEE SARA BEWITCHED HER HUSBAND!'

Victor's relatives insisted that Mee Sara explain to them what *muti* she had used to make him suffer like that for so long.

'Why didn't you just kill him instantly? Why did you have to make him suffer like that first?' they asked her.

The living room of the late Victor was packed with his relatives as they met to find out the cause of his death. They gathered around Mee Sara in a threatening and aggressive manner. They fired questions at her, questions that only confused her. It was heartbreaking. She looked like a frightened bird. Her face was wet with sweat, like a mother who was in labour, and her short fat body was curled up on the sofa as if she wanted to hide away from her in-laws. Her lips were so dry, they looked as if they'd been dipped in chalk. Once her eyes caught mine, asking for help. I cried. At that moment, I hated Michael's people. I hated them all. All of them! They behaved worse than children, like people devoid of understanding.

'You killed our relative,' they shouted at her.

'You are a murderer.'

Mee Sara denied causing her husband's death. 'I would never kill Victor, believe me. I had no reason to wish anything like that on him. You all know he was a good person,' she said and looked at their wedding picture on the wall. 'We were a happy couple.'

I looked at the picture, Victor carrying Mee Sara in his arms, an adorable sight. Victor say something, save your wife! I felt like screaming.

Despite her explanation, her in-laws were unconvinced. They insisted that she had killed Victor.

'If you think you killed our brother to inherit his wealth, you are greatly mistaken. We will show you a thing or two. '*Jy sal vokol kry nie*,'* one of Victor's cousins told Mee Sara. They stripped her of everything! Michael was so embarrassed that he complained.

'Please, people, let's behave like adults.'

'Michael, Michael. Don't disrespect us now,' one of them said.

'I don't disrespect anybody, but we must think of Mee Sara and the children as well.'

'You young people keep out of this. This is tradition. We know what we are doing.'

'Is this how you will treat my wife when I die?'

'We said, stay out of this!'

They dragged her to the bank to withdraw their relative's money. They took everything from the house, even the electronic appliances. I wondered how some of them would use them, as they did not have electricity in their homesteads. One of Victor's sisters, *a teacher*, mind you – you would think she would know better – 'inherited' the television set for her children. It was a mess.

---

* (In Afrikaans) 'You will get nothing.'

The Saturday after the funeral, Mee Sara's uncle, Tate Filli-pusa, announced that he had something very important to discuss with Victor's relatives before they departed. He asked to meet with Victor's closest relatives. He went straight to the point.

'There are people here who worked with and knew the late Victor very, very well. They told us something that I think you should all know,' he said with an angry frown on his face. He turned to a gentleman in a black suit, who stood to his left.

'Ericki, please, can you tell us again what you told us when we returned from the cemetery . . . About the disease . . . exactly as you told us then.' Erick was one of the men who had been introduced in the church as former colleagues of Victor. The man stepped forward as if he were going to deliver a speech.

'I know this is a family matter and we really don't want to interfere . . . However, my colleagues and I feel we have an obligation to clear up certain issues if we can,' Erick said, looking at his colleagues, who nodded in support and agreement.

'We knew Victor as a friend and as a colleague, until at least eight months ago. This is very hard for me to say . . .,' he went on, 'but Victor was not bewitched by his wife or anybody else. Victor was sick. He had this new disease called AIDS.' He scrutinised our faces. People looked at him as if he'd said that Victor was cursed. 'He was just sick. Sick like anybody who gets sick and dies from that disease. We know all this because once we had to go for a full medical check-up before we were able to work on the ocean in ships. Victor and three other colleagues were not selected. They were told that they could only work on shore as long as they were healthy. As soon as Victor got sick he was released from work and had to go home. We now understand that Mee Sara and his relatives did not know anything about Victor's disease. We are told that this disease makes people look different. Something none of us has never seen before. This is probably why some of you think he is bewitched. Victor is dead now and there is nothing we can do. However, what is important for us to know is that his death was not caused by any witchcraft. He was sick,' the young man concluded. I felt like applauding him. It was so quiet in the living room that it was hard to believe these were the same people who had ceaselessly harassed Mee Sara. They could not look at her.

'What you also told us at the cemetery, correct me if I am wrong . . . eh, you said that men get this disease when they sleep around,' Tate Fillipusa encouraged another discussion.

'Yes, partly, and through blood . . .'

'If that is the case . . .' Tate Fillipusa interrupted Erick, 'then if some of us here are honest with ourselves, we will not be surprised that Victor got this kind of a disease. We all know how he loved women. He chased every dress and skirt that passed him by. Now you people are sitting here accusing our child of bewitching your relative. Bewitching! Now, remember, when you say Sara bewitched your relative, you are actually saying the whole clan, we, here, us, *Aakuusinda*, also bewitch people,' he said forcefully, hitting his chest with his right hand, clearly angry. 'And don't forget one thing, Mee Sara, she is a corpse now, she is dying. She will die just like your relative, and all because of your . . .'

'Please, please Tate eh . . ., we don't know that for sure. This is a new disease for all of us and we need to learn more about it,' the colleague from the mine interrupted Tate Fillipusa before he got carried away.

Mee Sara's mother-in-law talked for the first time. 'Well, if this is the case then, Mee Sara, you are partly to blame for Victor's behaviour. I talked to you about that. Remember?' her mother-in-law asked. 'You allowed him to get away with murder. He impregnated other women – you didn't confront him. He did not sleep at home – you didn't confront him. He did not send you money – you didn't confront him. It did not matter what he did, you did not get angry with him. You spoiled him completely. If you had been a bit strict with him, he might not have been able to engage in the behaviour that led him to get the disease, which these people are now talking about. He would have still been here with you and the children,' Victor's mother said.

'I agree with you, Mother,' said Victor's sister, the teacher who inherited the television set. 'I remember Victor coming from the mine and spending his entire Easter weekend with friends at Oshakati without once going to Ongwediva to see his wife and children. But on his way back to the mine, he went to Mee Sara to ask for petrol money. Guess what she did? She gave it to him without a word.'

'You see, these are the things I am talking about, you were too soft with him and so you let him walk straight to his death.'

Somehow, Mee Sara found the courage to answer her in-laws. 'I complained about Victor's behaviour to you all, but every time I did this, you told me that he took after his father and grandfather. They too had more than one wife and many mistresses.' Mee Sara stated a truth which she knew they knew and one which they had never allowed to make a difference.

'One more thing,' Tate Fillipusa said. 'One more thing, before we go. Since you have stripped her of everything that belonged to your relative, Victor, we ask you to take her black clothes as well. She will not wear any of those mourning clothes. Why should she?'

'No, uncle, please,' Mee Sara protested feebly.

'We say, *no*! And you keep out of this,' Tate Fillipusa said,

107

giving Mee Sara a stern look. Mee Sara pulled her sweater against her chest as if she were suddenly cold and kept quiet.

◆

What will the Shanges do with Kauna? Will they take everything away from her too? Will they kick her off the land? If they don't think about Kauna, will they think about the children? If they ask her to go, where will she go? To Mee Fennie? To her parents? Where? I cannot imagine that they will throw her off the land, the land she loved and worked so hard on. The land that helped her to raise her children. The land she talked to so many times. The land she has shed tears and sweat on? Thinking about the land, I remember the time I helped her to organise *okakungungu* . . .

◆

It was a very hot day, not long before the rainy season, and when I saw Kauna and her children working in the field in the hot sun till afternoon, I walked over to greet them. I wondered if my friend would ever finish in time for the rains. After exchanging greetings, I spoke directly to her.

'My sister, I don't want to sound negative, but will you finish ploughing before the rains come? There is still a large piece of land left to do,' I said, looking at the vast area of uncultivated land.

'Well, I hope to finish . . .' she responded, but I could sense the uncertainty and concern in her voice.

'No, I don't think you will,' I said honestly. I was not sure if she would accept my proposal, but I suggested it to her anyway.

'Why don't you arrange for *okakungungu*?' I asked, somewhat hesitantly.

'*Okakungungu?*' Kauna asked, pulling a face.

'Yes, *okakungungu*. What is wrong with that?'

'Well, I don't know, it's just, it means I have to ask people.'

'But that is how it is done, asking people. How many times have you participated in *okakungungu*?'

'Many times, I guess . . .'

'So now what is wrong with people participating in yours?'

'I am not sure if I want to ask people to come and do my work.'

'Kauna, swallow your pride or whatever it is. Besides I don't think you have a choice,' I said, looking at the uncultivated land again.

'I wish my husband's people would help me, but you know how they are, they only work when Shange is here. They don't listen to me,' she said, holding the *etemo* with both her hands resting on the ground between her feet.

'Listen, Kauna, the rain is coming soon. It will not wait for you to finish ploughing and if you are not done by then, you will be the laughing stock of this village, not your husband or in-laws. It is also not fair to make the children work so hard in this heat while their friends are playing under the shade of the trees,' I said. Kauna looked at her children, the sweat shining on their tiny foreheads.

'How do I go about arranging for *okakungungu* if most of the women in the village don't like me?' she asked with her hand held shading her forehead to protect herself from the scorching sunlight.

'That is not true and you know it.'

'Will you help me then?'

'Of course, I will help you get all the women together and I promise you we will finish this field in one day,' I said hopefully.

'You think so?'

'Yes, I think so.'

'Thank you.'

'What are mothers for?' I said and tickled her side. She smiled.

'So what about a week from today? That will be next week Wednesday. It will give the women enough time to plan their activities.'

'What if they don't come?' Kauna asked, concerned.

'We invite as many as possible. We will start with your neighbours, the Shipangas.'

'Those people laughed at me when Shange beat me.'

'Let's invite them anyway. They are your neighbours. Then we move to the Shikongos.'

'Those people are friends with the woman from the white house.'

'Kauna, if you continue in this way, this one has said this about you and that one has done that, you will not accomplish anything. Kauna, you have helped people before, now it is their turn to help you. Allow them to do this.' She nodded.

'I will accompany you from house to house. What do you say?' She nodded again. But we both agreed on one thing, not to invite Mee Maita. I had never really forgiven her for breaking my confidence.

Kauna and I spent the next two days going from one homestead to the next in the village inviting women to take part in Kauna's *okakungungu*. At many, we were received with kindness and the promise that the householders would definitely participate. The last homestead we went to was Mukwankala's. Our visit to her was more of a courtesy call than an invitation as she was an old woman. Her homestead was just as clean as she was. Purple and white violets grew abundantly along the fence. We found her sitting on a straw mat, bare-breasted, busy applying red *olukula* lotion. She was red all over her face, arms and chest, her wrinkled breasts hung loose. For some reason, despite her strong Christian faith, *olukula* was one thing she would not give up. I never understood why – all the other Christians I knew would not apply *olukula*. She lightened up when she saw us. We stayed longer than we intended. One of her granddaughters served us *ontaku*. Kauna took hers with sugar, I didn't.

Mukwankala's favourite subject came up: her sons. 'I gave birth to nine boys. I hoped for a girl, one girl, just one girl, but not one,' she said, laughing. 'You know, when you have so many boys you worry all the time. What will become of them and that sort of a thing. Girls are OK. The only grief they bring is pregnancy before they are ready for it. But otherwise they try their best. You can rely on them. They are not likely to abandon you. I thank God most of my sons turned out well. Because there were no girls in our home, they had to do everything. They pounded, cooked, fetched water and wood. You must pray for your sons, Ali. Prayer kept me going,' she said, pointing at me.

'It is a good idea to have an *okakungungu*,' Mukwankala assured us repeatedly. 'Your *epya* is too big. If you don't finish it in time for the rains, people will talk about you, not about your husband.' She echoed my words.

'That is what I told her,' I said, looking at Kauna.

'Yes, my child, people will talk about you, that is how things are. You are a little late this year. Even Mee Helena, whom everybody says will always be behind like buttocks, has finished ploughing. She started earlier this year, now she is just waiting for the rain.'

The lazy bum of the village is waiting for the rain? Kauna thought, mouth open. I guess all the gossip had an effect.

'You must be strong, Kauna. Don't always walk around with your head hanging down. It is a pity your husband doesn't treat you well, but that should not allow you to feel sorry for yourself. Be strong and take care of yourself. I will come and see how you girls have worked.'

'Did you invite Mee Maita?' she asked. Kauna and I looked at each other. She dipped her index and middle finger in the small clay pot, which contained her *olukula* lotion. She rubbed it against her hands and applied to her upper arms and neck. Her skin looked beautifully smooth.

'Mee Maita didn't have much luck with her relationships,' Mukwankala said when we did not answer her question. 'The man she was supposed to marry dropped her at the last minute and married somebody else. She was shattered. She didn't want to have anything to do with men for years. I never really understood why. They are not all bad and she is a beautiful woman.'

She is beautiful indeed, I thought.

'She could have picked and chosen the man of her dreams at any time,' Mukwankala continued. 'Years later she probably realised that she was growing old and feared loneliness, so she started to "look". Friends and relatives found her Tate Ekandjo, a widower who, unfortunately, had never got over the death of his wife. Mee Maita couldn't handle the fact that her husband's heart belonged to another woman, a dead woman, a woman who did not bear him any children. The more she complained, the more he resorted to alcohol. Nowadays we all know that alcohol is his companion. It is very hard for her,' Mukwankala advised us gently.

From Mukwankala we went straight to Mee Maita. It was the first time I had set foot in her house since my famous visit three years previously. She was pleasantly surprised to see us. I was a bit nervous.

'I need to lay a stone for you to step on,' she said, sounding genuine. She led us to the same room that we had sat in. Memories of that visit flashed back. Our eyes met. 'I am happy to have you both in our house,' she said, 'truly, I am.' She was even happier when we informed her of the reason for our visit.

'*Okakungungu* is a good idea. If you don't finish in time for the rain, people will talk about you, not your in-laws.' She shared Mukwankala's sentiment. 'People will say what a lazy, useless wife you are. They will accuse you of making your husband poor,' she continued in a sisterly manner that I had never seen before. I was not sure if I could handle another meal. She understood and offered us *ontaku* and a live chicken each.

We had completed the first phase of *okakungungu*. Kauna went to all her neighbours and asked for *omatemos* and so she completed the second phase. The third phase was the cooking.

'What will you slaughter?' I asked her.

'A goat, my biggest goat,' she said, excited.

All day Tuesday until late in the afternoon, Kauna and I cooked and brewed *omalovu* for the *okakungungu* day. As usual, my daughter, Kauna, enjoyed doing things for her name-sake, and together with Kauna's daughters, the girls all had fun helping us. There was plenty of food. It looked as if we were going to feed the whole village. We prepared *oshithima* as the main dish and a variety of others to go with it: spinach, chicken, goat, beans, milk and dried caterpillars – a delicacy. I brewed *omalovu*. I was considered the expert.

I prepared the sorghum flour and mixed it with water in a huge pot. I stirred the mixture well. I put the pot on the fire and continued to stir. I kept the fire low to prevent over-cooking and burning. When a reddish foam appeared on the surface of the mixture, it was ready. I removed the pot from the fire to cool off. I poured the ingredients of sorghum and water from the pot into a corn bag for filtering. It was a slow process. It took the whole night. I poured the filtered liquid into a calabash. I dug a hole in the earth and put the calabash into it.

Then I half filled the hole. This helped to keep the contents warm and helped to speed up the fermentation process.

In the morning, the *omalovu* was ready. I added two handfuls of freshly pounded *omahangu* flour to add a fresh flavour.

Before the cocks crowed and the dawn had broken, the women of Oshaantu were already at the Shanges. Kauna ululated to welcome the women. She praised them as they lifted their *omatemo*.

'*Mweya aashona, mweya aashona,*
Iyaloo aakadhona yandje, iyaloo.'*

The women responded to her welcome and praise songs. Kauna and I were pleasantly surprised by the high turnout. My concern about whether *okakungungu* would be a success was quickly forgotten. Almost all the women we had invited came. Mee Maita came and Sustera came too. Somehow Mee Namutenya, Tate Oiva's crazy ex-wife, heard about Kauna's *okakungungu* and invited herself. She sang of how hard she used to work on her husband's land, how she used to be the first wife to finish ploughing before the rains came, how she used to feed her mother-in-law, how she made him feel proud of her and how she made him rich, how she did this and that for him and his clan.

Most surprisingly, Kauna's 'arch enemy' also came, a woman who had apparently said that Kauna was barren because of some Depo contraceptive. 'Who would want to stay in bed when you girls are singing so beautifully?' she announced with her *etemo* in her hands.

'Yes, aren't they singing beautifully?' Kauna replied.

'I didn't know you knew the praise songs so well,' I said to Kauna and pinched her on her left buttock.

'Oh, don't you underestimate me, woman, it was not all

* 'You came, few of you.
Great my daughters, great!'

114

praying and Bible reading in my father's house. We consulted with our ancestors too, you know.'

'Oh . . .' I said, widening my eyes, acting shocked. She laughed. I had never seen Kauna in such a relaxed and happy mood. I stood still to embrace this rare mood. I always thought she had an innocent beauty. I must have been staring at her.

'What?'

'What, what?'

'Why are you looking at me like that?'

'You are a beautiful woman.'

'What?'

'Forget it,' I said, but you should have seen her face!

We worked and worked.

We worked with one spirit.

We worked as if we competed for a prize.

We sang in harmony.

When we finished one song, the women would start another one.

We sang all kinds of songs:

Songs of our ancestors,

frightening songs,

songs of sorrow,

songs of joy,

songs of forgiveness,

songs of unity and hope.

When we did not sing, the *omatemos* did. We let the music of the *omatemos* take their course, loud and clear.

'We call on our ancestors, our great-grandmothers,' one of the women called and the rest of us confirmed. We called on them . . .

'Wake up and look at us.'

'Yes wake up . . .'

'Wake up and watch our bent backs.'

'Yes wake up.'

'Wake up and look how hard we work.'

'Yes wake up . . .'

'Wake up and join your granddaughters.'

'Yes wake up . . .'

'Wake up and bless us.'

'Yes wake up . . .'

'Wake up!'

'Yes wake up . . .'

'Wake up!'

'Yes wake up, yes wake up, yes wake up!'

The women understood Kauna's situation. There was a wonderful spirit, a spirit of sisterhood. For once, all ill-feeling and hate were forgotten. We were one again, sisters sharing a common cause.

The sun kept its promise and slowly lifted into the sky, gently stroking our naked shoulders with its beautiful yellow and orange colours. A new day. The birds were calling, screaming and shouting. It was not their usual soothing music. They sounded annoyed. It was as if we had trespassed on their territory. We continued to work. When the girls brought us *ontaku*, we took a break for about half an hour. We got back to work. Last was Kauna's piece of land at the edge of her husband's land. With our backs bent we worked. The afternoon intensified with the heat. Sweat dripped down our faces and backs, but we worked, we continued to plough.

'It is so hot! The sun is unbearable,' I complained.

'We are about to finish,' Sustera encouraged me.

'Sisters, sisters, we can leave my piece of land, it's OK as long as we have finished the . . .'

'*No!*' the women roared. 'We will finish yours too.'

Sustera impressed me most. Without her uniform, she looked

just like one of us. Her back bent, she moved skilfully, forward, working. She was absolutely wonderful.

At last we finished! Finished. We went to sit under the big *marula* tree. We literally threw ourselves on the ground. The girls were ready to serve us. We enjoyed our well-deserved food and drinks. We became loud and talkative with much help from the *omalovu*. We cracked jokes and told many, many stories. Stories that brought us closer together.

All of a sudden the crazy Mee Namutenya jumped up. 'So, what if we had not all come to Kauna's *okakungungu*, what if we had all decided to stay away so that Shange's field would not be cultivated this year? I'll tell you, the people of Oshaantu would have gossiped about Kauna, saying that she is a "useless wife". They would have accused her of making her husband poor, so that when Shange came from the mine and found that his land was not cultivated, he would have beaten Kauna and maybe this time he would have killed her. What if we had not come here today?' The crazy woman acted as if she were telling children a scary story. One of the older women jumped up to reprimand Mee Namutenya sternly.

'*Satana, zapo! Satana, zapo!*'* she cried and made as if to chase Mee Namutenya away. Looking around, I could see that people were divided. Some felt Mee Namutenya was 'mad' and were afraid of her, not only because of what she said, but because of the way she looked; others, perhaps reluctantly, felt that there was a lot of truth in her words, and I was one of those. It seemed all wrong that she should have to beg for forgiveness and promise not to make any trouble, before she was allowed to stay. She gave me a quiet smile. My heart went out to Mee Namutenya as I looked at her worn and filthy appearance.

* 'Satan, go away! Satan, go away!'

117

Our party resumed. Mee Karina stood up, holding her *oshi-tenga* in her left hand and pointing at us with her right hand.

'Ladies, ladies. Let us remember our husbands who are very, very far, who are working far, on the mines, on the farms, on the . . .' she started and stopped suddenly. 'Sustera, where does your husband work again?'

'Walvis Bay, in the fish factory,' she said. Sustera had drunk a lot of *omalovu*, but she was not loud like the rest of us.

'And those who work in the fish factories,' Mee Karina continued.

'And beer factories,' another woman added.

'Yes and those who work in beer factories. We pray for them, to work hard and we promise that we shall keep the fire burning for their safety and good luck.' The women nodded in agreement.

'Yes, we shall keep the fire burning . . .'

'And also they should not sleep around and take second wives,' a young woman who had been married for about a year added with strong emphasis, pointing her index finger above her head and burping very loudly.

'*Ombili*,' she said. She burped again.

'*Ombili*,' she said.

'You really are not a lady,' one of the women said.

The young woman burped again. '*Ombili*,' she said.

'Stop saying "excuse me", you don't mean it,' another woman scolded her. Kauna found the situation extremely funny and laughed from her belly. Her laugh was contagious. We all laughed.

Most of our husbands, in fact most able young men, worked hundreds of kilometres away from home. Except for the headman and a few older men, this village was headed, literally, by us, the women.

Mukwankala arrived amidst the noise. She went to have a

look at what we had done, as if inspecting work done by her employees. With her hands folded behind her back, she took her time scrutinising our labour. She dug her toes in the sand a couple of times. We were still, following her movements with our eyes. She seemed satisfied. She looked at us and smiled.

I wanted to run towards all those women, and hug and kiss them all. I wished the spirit would last forever among us. Although this *okakungungu* lasted just one day, a feeling of sisterhood and communal responsibility enveloped us in a strange and cheerful sense of oneness. I felt connected to these women, these sisters, these mothers, these aunts, and grand-mothers. As we parted, I looked at them and thought, Yes, girls, you have done it again.

Chapter Nine

Kauna and I were quiet, listening to the sound of a car coming towards the homestead.

'More people,' I said to Kauna when the car stopped outside. A few minutes later, Mee Sofia came in to inform Kauna that her people had arrived. At last! I thought.

Mee Sofia asked me to accompany her and escort Kauna's relatives to her hut. They must have left their village very early to have arrived by now. It's only about nine o'clock, I thought as I looked at the sun.

I didn't know what to expect from her parents, especially her mother. I wondered how she was reacting to the death of her son-in-law. People started to cry when I hugged Kauna's mother. I shook hands with the other relatives. I didn't understand why people cried so much when they saw Kauna's family. They didn't know them! What emotions could they possibly evoke? I wondered.

'Let me know when they are ready to settle down. Their rooms are ready,' Mee Sofia said.

'I will do so, Mee Sofia,' I replied. I was happy that she had arranged accommodation for Kauna's people. I had been worried that if I had done this, I would have been seen as interfering in her marriage again. Mee Sofia is a good person, very organised and hardworking. She has never troubled Kauna, but she has also never said anything about her cousin treating his wife badly.

I led Kauna's people to her hut. It was a large group of about eleven people – neighbours, friends and extended family. The last time I had seen Kauna's mother was on a visit she had made about five years previously. She had grown much older since then. I didn't know what I thought Mee Fennie would look like. Although she resembled her sister in features, she was much taller and darker in complexion. Kauna's mother, Meme Maria, and Kauna's aunt, Meme Fennie, were the first to enter the hut. As soon as they saw Kauna, they all started to cry. The three women, Kauna, Mee Maria and Mee Fennie, formed a circle as they embraced one another and cried. They cried as if there were no end to their tears. Kauna cried for the first time. I cried again. What made us cry so much?

'We are sorry we couldn't come right away. We had problems getting a vehicle,' they apologised.

'It's OK, Meme, Mee Ali was here with me all the time,' she said.

'Oh yes, yes,' Mee Fennie said as if she had just remembered something very important. She put both her hands on her chest.

'My child, we have heard how supportive and helpful you were to our child. I, especially, cannot thank you enough.'

'It is all right, she is "my daughter" too and I will do whatever I can to help her. It's OK really, don't worry,' I assured her. Mee Maria turned to her daughter.

'Your father couldn't come with us. He can only come on Friday. He is very busy right now,' she said. Kauna's mother and aunt sat on the bed.

'You don't look like people who have travelled a long journey. You look so fresh and dressed up,' Kauna remarked. Her mother looked at her sister accusingly as if to say, 'It was her idea.' Mee Fennie wore a light-blue two-piece suit with a colourful blouse to match her outfit and a church hat with reddish feathers. Mee Maria wore a green traditional *ontulo*

121

dress with butterfly designs and a headscarf of the same material.

'Well, I told your mother that we should look present-able. These people haven't been treating you well and we don't want to give them any reasons to justify that,' Mee Fennie explained.

'She even told your uncle Samwele not to come with us,' Mee Maria added.

'No, Mee Fennie, you didn't,' Kauna said in disbelief.

'Yes, child, I did. My daughter, you know his drinking problem. He was just going to get drunk and disgrace all of us. I think it is better that he stayed behind. But your favourite uncle Peetu is here,' she said smiling.

'What happened?' her mother asked her gently. Kauna explained the whole story to her attentive mothers. I thought it wise to leave Kauna alone with her mother and aunt. I wandered through the homestead that now looked something like a refugee camp. Mourners were everywhere as they increased with daily arrivals. Temporary huts, serving as bedrooms and kitchens, had been erected. Some, the young especially, had made their beds in the open space. Somebody had brought a tent. It was a commotion of people. It didn't look like Shange's house at all.

◆

'How are they treating you?' Mee Fennie asked.

'Who? My in-laws?' Kauna asked and answered her own question.

'Yes, your in-laws. Are they not accusing you of killing your husband?'

'Fennie! Please stop it,' Mee Maria reprimanded her sister.

'Stop what?' she asked with obvious irritation.

'This is not the place or time to ask such questions,' she said, looking at Kauna for support. Kauna looked away.

'How have they been?' Mee Fennie asked again, ignoring her sister.

'Well, yesterday they called me and Mee Ali to a clan meeting to explain the sudden and "mysterious" death of my husband. They think I killed Shange and they believe that I know where his wealth is and that I should give it all back to them,' Kauna told her aunt and mother.

'I knew they would imagine you killed your husband, but to think you know anything about his money and cattle is ludicrous,' Mee Fennie said, talking with her whole body. Mee Maria constantly had to remind her to lower her voice.

'There is something else. Ali told me they are angry because I am not crying . . .'

'You are not?' the two women called out almost simultaneously.

'Shhh,' Kauna said. 'No, I am not crying . . .'

'No, no, no. You must cry,' her mother said firmly. Mee Fennie rose up from the bed.

'Child, are you sure? Mee Fennie prompted, clearly taken aback by Kauna's attitude.

'Yes, yes, Mother, I am sure,' Kauna said, clenching her tiny fist and looking at both her mother and aunt.

'This is dangerous, you know,' Mee Fennie said again.

'Yes, I know.'

'*Ntowele*, whatever you decide to do, we will support you,' Mee Fennie said, looking at her sister for confirmation. Mee Maria did not say another word. It was hard to tell if she was shocked, surprised or angry with her daughter.

'Child, do you need anything? I think we may want to go to Ondangwa tomorrow to buy a few things for ourselves,' Mee Fennie informed Kauna.

'*Yakwetu*, Fennie, what do you need to buy again? You carried the whole house with you, emptied all the stores, and as a result we didn't have enough sitting space in the car,' Mee Maria burst out.

'What did you bring?' Kauna asked, curious.

'Food and other important goods.'

'I think we brought enough with us and I really don't think we need any more.'

'I am going to Ondangwa tomorrow. We cannot just sit here and use the little that Kauna has or what the Shanges have bought. You know how people talk. When we leave this village we don't want people to forget our names and refer to us as the ones who came empty-handed and finished everything off.'

'We did not come empty-handed!'

'If you don't need anything, Kauna and I do,' she said, looking at Kauna for support.

'For now I am fine, Mother. The Shanges have taken care of everything already. Thanks again to Mee Ali. I don't know what I would have done without her. She has been my pillar since I came to this village.'

'I like her spirit. She has a good spirit,' Mee Fennie said.

'She has,' Kauna agreed.

'We have transport. We hired a car . . .'

'Which will cost me all my money and all your cattle,' Mee Maria said with an unhappy expression on her face.

'Mother, Mother, please . . .,' Kauna warned her mothers when she sensed that an argument was about to start that had to do with hiring the car.

'You have black clothes to wear for the funeral and afterwards, don't you?' Mee Maria asked.

'My husband was very superstitious about the colour black. As a result I never wore anything black.'

'What?' Mee Fennie exclaimed, shocked.

124

'Yes, he would ask me "Whom are you mourning?" or "Do you want me dead?"'

'You see! These are the things I am talking about. We need to go to Ondangwa and buy such things,' she said, giving her sister an accusing look.

'Thank you, Mother, but Shange's relatives from Windhoek said that they would take care of my clothes, the children's and all his other children's.'

'Oh' is all Mee Fennie said.

'One more thing. I am going to say something on behalf of our clan. Something short, just to thank everyone for supporting you and the children during this time,' Mee Fennie announced. Mee Maria seemed bothered that her sister had appointed herself spokesperson for the family, but she said nothing. Mee Fennie claims that she always does this, 'otherwise things don't get done'. Finally, Uncle Peetu and the rest of the delegation were given a chance to express their sympathy. Uncle Peetu kissed Kauna on her lips and cried openly. Mee Fennie rolled her eyes as if to say, 'This brother of mine'. We all knew she was fond of him, but his manners exasperated her.

Kauna comforted him. Kuku Peetu has always been her favourite uncle. He was gentle and often shy, but he loved to dress flamboyantly and he had a 'style'.

◆

After about two hours of wandering around the Shanges' homestead, I returned to Kauna's hut to see if they were ready to settle down. Mee Sofia had arranged three huts for them, two for the ladies and one for the men. I led them to their huts. Mourners watched the delegation curiously as they carried their goods one by one into the huts.

'Mee Fennie looks like a together person,' I said to Kauna.

'Oh yes, she is. She has just appointed herself spokesperson for the family.'

'She has?'

'Yes, she has.' We both laughed, putting our hands on our mouths so we didn't make any noise.

'When she divorced her husband, the village people and all the prophets of doom, including her own relatives, predicted her downfall and her children starving. Nothing like that happened. She put her first daughter through high school and she is now at the University of Namibia studying administration. Her other daughter and son are both doing well. I sometimes wish she was my mother or at least that mother was a bit more like her.'

'But she is also your mother. Remember your mother's sister is also your mother.'

'Yes, but still I cannot help but wonder what my life would have been like if she had been my birth mother.'

'I think I like Mee Fennie too,' I said after a while.

'I knew you would like her. She is like you in many ways.'

'Like me?' I asked, surprised.

'Yes, she is like you. She is your type. You are very much like her.'

'Well, I don't know about that. Mee Fennie seems to stand so tall and strong . . . confident, full of guts . . .'

'And you are not like that?'

Chapter Ten

A little after midday, I decided to go home. 'I am sure Kauna's people and the Shanges will be fine without me,' I thought.

As I walked home I caught sight of children who were supposed to be looking after the cattle but seemed instead to be playing. They would be in big trouble if their beasts wandered off into other people's *mahangu* fields.

'It's a humid day,' I reflected as I entered our homestead. The many beautiful purple and white violets along the fence, which I notice at times, reminded me of my husband, who would often call me '*kangala*' when he was in a jovial mood.

My children had returned from school. They were preparing their lunch – *oshithima* with milk. My daughter held her baby brother in her arms.

'Careful, Kauna, he will mess your uniform,' I warned her.

'It's OK, Meme,' she said, but held him away from her body after peeping at his dusty buttocks.

'How often have I told you to take your uniform off as soon as you get home?' I asked, walking to our bedroom without waiting for an answer.

'I was going to take it off . . .'

My third son, the eight-year-old Kangulu, is known to be a little informer and so he is not very popular with his brothers and sister. Whenever they do something they do not want us to hear about, they make sure he does not pick up a word of it. He talks too much. I usually get information from him about everything that goes on at school and at home.

127

'It is not good to talk in this way. You are not a woman,' I warn him at times when I think he talks too much nonsense. People say he takes after me. I definitely think he takes after his father's people. They talk too. But sometimes he has important information – information that, were it not for his little big mouth, I would not know anything about.

'Michael is sleeping,' Kangulu informed me.

'Sleeping? Sleeping at this time of the day? Is he sick?'

Kangulu lowered his voice. 'He wrote a letter to Ngonyofi and put fifty cents in the envelope.'

'What letter?'

'That he wants her to be his girl. Ngonyofi gave the letter with its fifty cents to her friend Kasape to give it back to Michael. Kasape found Michael and his friends playing soccer and she just started to talk, to talk-talk like a bird, in front of everybody, saying, "*Michael, aniwa Ngonyofi okwa ti, iithilinga itano mbino ka lande owala omikuki dhoye komatala.*" * Everybody heard Kasape. They laughed at Michael. Now everybody at school knows that Michael wanted Ngonyofi to be his girl and she rejected him and his fifty cents. Michael left school during the tea break and did not return.' Kangulu's little fat fingers moved like a music conductor's as he gossiped about his brother. I decided to go over to Michael's hut.

'Michael, are you not well? Why are you sleeping this time of the day?'

'I have a headache.'

'Shall I bring you a tablet?'

'I will be fine soon.'

I didn't know what to do. It must be humiliating for him. What do I tell him? Should I pretend I had not heard about the Ngonyofi story or tell him that I knew and that he should not

* Nognyofi apparently said, 'Michael take your fifty cents and go and buy fat cakes at the street market!'

worry? Where did he find fifty cents anyway? I decided to let things be for a bit. I returned to the kitchen. The children were all sitting on the ground, eating. Kangulu avoided my eyes, as if he felt guilty that he had betrayed his brother.

'What is for lunch?' I asked, though I could see what they were eating.

'*Oshithima* and milk. Do you want some, Meme?' Kauna asked.

'No, thank you, maybe later.' I decided to take a nap. Minutes later I heard somebody at the bedroom door.

'Mammy . . .' My daughter stood at the entrance of the hut.

'Come in, come in.'

'Mammy . . .,' she said again.

'Yes, Kauna, I am listening. What is bothering my only girl?' I encouraged her to talk.

'What are they going to do with my *mbushe*?' she asked. I had completely forgotten about her. Shange's death must have affected her too in some way. He is her *mbushe*'s husband.

'What do you mean, what are they going to do with your *mbushe*?' I asked her, not sure how to handle her question.

'Are they going to chase her away from the homestead?'

'Why would they chase her from the homestead?'

'I heard . . . they say . . . because she bewitched Tate Shange.'

'Where did you hear that?'

'At school.'

'Come here, come sit here.' I invited her to sit on the bed. 'Do you believe that your *mbushe* would do something like that? That she would bewitch anybody?'

'No, no, I don't believe that my *mbushe* would bewitch anybody. Maybe some people would bewitch other people, but not my *mbushe*,' she said with certainty.

'If they ask her to leave the homestead, it will not be because they think your *mbushe* bewitched Tate Shange, but because that is how some people do certain things,' I explained to her, stroking her back gently.

'But whose land is it then, Mammy?' she asked with a confused frown and the innocence of a child. The question caught me by surprise, but I told her what I had to tell her.

'It is Tate Shange's land . . .'

'But Tate Shange is dead now and he never worked on that land. It was always just my *mbushe* who did that!' she said, clenching her fists in protest.

'Kauna, my daughter, you are still too young to understand these things, but one day when you are a grown woman, you will understand, OK?'

She nodded. I was not sure if she was satisfied with my explanation, but soon after she had left I went to look for my mother-in-law. I found her sitting under the *omuye* tree weaving a basket. She wore an old skirt that had not seen water and soap for some time. She was bare-chested. Her breasts hung loose. Her wrinkles told untold stories about the many years of her life. Her hair that I cut and keep short for her was entirely grey. I sat beside her on a straw mat. The huge *omuye* tree exposing its giant roots provided wonderful shade and a cool breeze.

'I did not come today,' she said, apologising for not going to the mourning house.

'Oh, Mother, don't bother. That house is so full today, nobody noticed your absence. Besides, Kauna's people arrived this morning and are now the centre of all attention.'

'They did? What took them so long? Three days?'

'I think it is a long story.'

Satisfied, she proceeded to greet me formally.

'*Owu hala po ngaa nawa.*'*

* 'Good day.'

130

'*Ee.*'*

'*Onawa tuu?*'†

'*Ee.*'

I returned her greetings. '*Ne omwa lala po tuu.*'‡

'*Ee.*'

'*Onawa tuu?*'

'*Ee.*'

She straightened her legs, took up her basket and continued to weave it. She does this so naturally, it seems as if she can weave in the dark.

'You must look after yourself,' she said suddenly and continued to weave, her hands still moving strongly.

'I will, Mother,' I said after some moments.

'It is very easy to neglect yourself during times like this,' she said.

'You are right, mother,' I said, feeling suddenly tired. I appreciated her concern.

Sometimes I wondered if this was the same woman who once couldn't stand me. She had changed over the years and helped me to raise my children. She never apologised for the manner in which she first treated me, but I suspect that she has regretted it.

She once suffered from malaria. We all feared for her death. She lost weight, shook like a feather and sweated continuously. I suggested that she change her bed and atmosphere and come and stay with us. 'It helps to recuperate faster,' I said. Sustera was a great help. She provided me with all sorts of tips for taking care of a malaria patient. I spoiled the old woman. I did that for two reasons. First, I really wanted her to get better; second, I wanted to prove to her that I was not such a bad

* A form of acknowledgement.
† 'Is it fine?'
‡ 'Good day to you.'

daughter-in-law after all. It paid off. She has since referred to me as her angel, the one who brought her back to life.

When she was well again, she plainly stated that she wanted to live with Michael and his wife and grandchildren. That was almost five years ago. Of course there have been ups and downs in our relationship, but they are more like those of a mother and daughter than a mother and daughter-in-law. We mainly disagree over our manner of bringing up our children. Sometimes she thinks I am too strict and sometimes too lenient with her grandchildren. But she is good company in the absence of Michael or Kauna.

It was the first time since Shange's death that I had slept at home. I couldn't sleep. It was everything. The bed was too big. I missed my husband. Shange had died. I wanted to cry, but my tears were stuck somewhere. The mosquitoes bothered me. It was hot! I tossed and turned in the darkness. It felt that, except for the crickets, I was the only one awake. It seemed a long time till dawn.

'Goodbye, Mammy.' One by one my kids attended me before leaving for school.

'Goodbye,' I said, still groggy. My eyes felt heavy.

'Michael is not going to school,' Kangulu whispered and disappeared. I dragged myself out of bed and over to my son's hut.

'Michael, why are you not going to school? Do you still have a headache?' I asked him gently.

'Yes,' he said.

'Michael, I heard what happened at school yesterday between you and Ngonyofi. Is this the reason that you are not going to school?' Michael pulled the blanket over his head.

'I know how you feel and the students will probably tease you for some time, but the pain will go away. You will make it worse if you don't go to school today. The children will know that you are absent because of the letter you wrote to Ngonyofi. Do our clan members run away from problems?' I asked him. He shook his head.

'Don't run away. Go and face them. It will be easier in the long run,' I said and left him. Michael is only thirteen. This incident made me realise that he was growing into a young man. I was not sure how to handle the emotions that accompanied his growth. It was at times like these that I wished my husband was at home with us. I felt helpless.

'Goodbye, Mom,' he said a while later, trying hard to hold up his head.

'Goodbye, *Shiveli*, and hurry. Be strong, eh?' I called after him. My heart went out to him. Kids can really be little devils, and so cruel to each other sometimes!

◆

I wished Michael came to see us more often. Sometimes I worry about bringing the children up on my own. Life is changing fast, even in our little village, and it is sometimes hard to know what to do, and how to respond. More often than not, I think I get it wrong.

I thought about my husband. He is a good man. I was reminded of a story he told me years after we had married about his friend Jacopo, who had helped him to find his first job and had invited him to stay in his family home.

Jacopo had married a woman, Mee Nangula, now so successful that she owns several supermarkets. But life had been hard to her. And Jacopo had been hard on her, and all because of his jealous relatives.

Jacopo had a job far away in Luderitz as a fisherman and his wife owned a small shop, which was well situated, close to the church, clinic and school. Students were her best customers.

Mee Nangula was not only hard-working, she was helpful and friendly. 'Almost flirtatious,' Michael had told me, smiling as he remembered her. 'She knew exactly how to turn her customers around her small finger.'

But as her business grew, so did jealousy and gossip. Why, there was even a malicious rumour that Michael and she were sleeping together. I had been shocked when he told me this. I had felt a twinge of jealousy. But Michael would certainly not sleep with his best friend's wife. I know this, even though I did not know him at the time.

Matters had got worse and Michael had been caught in the middle, although he had left Jacopo's house as soon as he had heard the rumours. Nonetheless, he lived in the same town as Jacopo's in-laws and they had fed him with stories about Mee Nangula's 'wickedness': she wouldn't let them use the car whenever they wanted, she wouldn't give them free goods from the store, she wouldn't tell them how much money she had made, she had employed a domestic worker and didn't do her own cooking any more, and so on. While he felt loyalty to Jacopo and his relatives who had offered him a home, he could see that Mee Nangula was doing a professional job, and that she too was very unhappy.

To her it seemed that Jacopo's relatives wanted everything free and her husband wouldn't stand up for her. 'It seemed,' Michael told me, 'that loyalty to relatives was more important than loyalty to one's wife. This taught me an important lesson. One I have never forgotten.'

Eventually, Jacopo's relatives accused her of witchcraft. Jacopo returned from Luderitz, gave up his well-paying fishing job and told Mee Nangula that he would run the store by himself, without her. Of course, to cut a long and painful story short, his own relatives bled him dry. The shop went bankrupt and Mee Nangula tired of all the insults, the demoralisation and her husband's complete lack of support, and she left him. She went on to do well, very well. But poor Jacopo had never managed to pick up the pieces.

Michael had told me this story a long time ago, and I wondered why I was thinking about it again, now. Shange's relatives were certainly not supporting their daughter-in-law. What would happen if I died? And my mind went full circle and I wished Michael were with me at times like these. He could see things clearly.

Chapter Eleven

My mother-in-law and I stayed at home all morning, observing the happenings at the mourning house from our homestead. I slaughtered a chicken for lunch to surprise the children. They were pleasantly surprised: such treats are not for every day. Michael junior looked better. It looked as if the Ngonyofi saga at school was over.

'How is the man of the house doing, hmm?' I asked, rubbing his head. He smiled shyly.

After lunch my mother-in-law and I went to the mourning house. I greeted a few relatives and went straight to Kauna's hut. I found her with her mother and some of the people who had come with them. Despite the fact that Kauna had assured Mee Fennie that she did not need anything, Mee Fennie had driven to Ondangwa early in the morning.

'I will leave you girls now. I want to lie down a bit,' Kauna's mother said and stood up. The others made their excuses and left.

'I think they just wanted us to be alone,' I told Kauna. She smiled. About an hour later, Mee Kiito, Shange's first cousin, came to the hut. She bent her head and squeezed her short fat body through the hut opening. She held a pen and a note pad in her right hand.

'How is our poor widow doing today?' she greeted us, out of breath, and put both her hands on her hips, tired. She has a big tummy that always makes her look pregnant. Obviously she did not tie her stomach properly, and for long enough, with a leather belt after the birth of her baby.

'Ah, so so, my dear Mee Kiito. What can we say? We must just pray for strength during this difficult time,' I responded, trying to sound as sad as I could, but at the same time wondering if she really cared how Kauna felt. After exchanging greetings with both Kauna and me, she explained to us that she would be the Mistress of Ceremonies at the church for the funeral ceremony.

'I am putting a list of names together so that Mr Jackson can prepare the programme for the funeral service. Names of speakers, who will carry the coffin, the choirs, the hymns, who will do this and that on Saturday. He wants everything to be ready by tomorrow, Friday, so that he can have it typed and photocopied. He has told us that he does not want to run around on Saturday morning. You know how he is,' she explained, laughing as if she had just remembered something about Mr Jackson that tickled her. She bent over Kauna, who still lay on the bed with her hands behind her head.

'Have you identified somebody who will read your speech for you in church?' Mee Kiito asked Kauna, and looked at me as if I might be a candidate.

'What speech?' Kauna asked.

'What do you mean, "what speech"? Will you not have somebody say something on your behalf, about your husband, as all widows do?' Mee Kiito replied, surprised.

'Oh that. No, I will not have anybody say anything on my behalf. There is nothing to be said,' Kauna said quietly, as if she really appreciated the invitation but for reasons beyond her control could not avail herself to do anything.

'What?' Mee Kiito exclaimed, shocked.

'My small mother will say something on behalf of my clan. Her name is Fennie Nangolo. You can write that down,' she said.

'But I am not asking on behalf of your clan, I am talking on behalf of *you*, the widow. Don't you understand me?'

'Yes, Mee Kiito, I understand what you are saying, but there will be no speech on behalf of *me*, the widow,' Kauna retorted. Mee Kiito's big nostrils flared as she tried to control her emotions. She breathed heavily. For a split second I thought she would do something to Kauna. She looked as if she could hit her.

'You are doing this on purpose, aren't you?' Mee Kiito said with forced calmness. 'You want to disgrace our clan. You want to demonstrate to the whole world what a horrible man my cousin was. You want this, is that not so? Haven't you done enough damage to his name already by running around like a crazy freak broadcasting, for everybody to hear, that Shange had not slept at home the night before he died? I feel sorry for you, terribly sorry,' Mee Kiito went on with a cynical laugh.

'Mee Kiito, please . . .,' I intervened when I realised that something nasty was about to unfold, and I stood up and somehow positioned myself between the bed and Mee Kiito. 'Mee Kiito, I am sure this is something that can be taken care of easily. Let me talk to Mee Fennie,' I continued, smiling, hoping to ease the tension in the atmosphere. She looked at me as if she was not happy that I had interrupted in time to stop the argument. She left with the promise that she would come back later. We listened to her departing footsteps. Immediately I turned to Kauna.

'I am going to kill you. Are you crazy? What do you think you are doing?'

'You are not going to kill me and I am not crazy. I am serious. There will be no speeches on behalf of the widow.'

'No, no, you are not serious,' I said, swinging my index finger

138

in front of her face. 'Have you thought of the consequences of your behaviour?' She nodded.

'My God, Kauna, you are scaring me.'

'Ali, whatever I do, whether I faint or cry on top of my lungs so that I lose my voice and say how "wonderful" a husband Shange was, they will still do what they will do,' Kauna answered. I sighed deeply. What a mess, I thought.

'But, Ali, can you imagine what I have to say about that man? Can you picture me saying . . . No! I am not going to tell the lies that widows tell at their husbands' funerals. I am not going to say what an honourable, loving and faithful husband he was, while everybody in the village knows what type of a man he was. No, I will not make a laughing stock of myself. No, not because of Shange or anyone else,' she said with finality. 'Shange does not even expect me to do this.' I realised that Kauna had made up her mind and that nothing would change it.

'You are putting me in an awkward situation. Your in-laws will think I have something to do with your decision,' I said, worried.

◆

The hut felt too small when Mee Kiito returned. I wanted to hide. She was away for at least three hours, but it felt like three minutes. I felt caught in the middle of a situation. I swore I had nothing to do with it. I thought of my husband. I had promised him never to interfere in the Shanges' marriage problems.

'I have not changed my mind. I still stand by my decision. I will not say anything at the funeral. I think it is better this way,' Kauna said bravely, looking at Mee Kiito.

'Why are you being so disrespectful towards Shange? Over

the last few years or so, he did not lift his finger to hurt you,' she said, almost pleading. Kauna said nothing.

Mee Kiito lifted her chin. 'Well, I am not going to argue with you, if this is what you want . . .' She pointedly shrugged her shoulders.

'I want you all to know that this is my decision and my decision alone. Nobody is behind it,' Kauna continued. Mee Kiito looked at me.

'Bed open up and swallow me up!' I felt like screaming. Mee Kiito stood still, scrutinising Kauna and me, as if deciding what to do next. She looked at me again, then at Kauna, and cast me a last look before, without another word, she left the hut.

Quietness fell between my friend and me until we heard more footsteps approaching. We sat very still, just as we had every time we had heard somebody coming towards Kauna's hut over the last few days. Tate Salomo, Shange's elder brother, announced his presence before he reached the entrance. His long legs were still trotting outside the door long after we had concluded the greetings. I was about to invite him in, when he asked, 'May I come in please . . . ?'

'Oh, oh, trouble,' I whispered to Kauna. 'Ee, come in please.' I invited him in, tidying the bed quickly.

Mee Kiito has informed him that Kauna has refused to prepare a speech for her husband's funeral. Now he is going to threaten Kauna and tell her to do it or face the consequences, I thought, feeling my heart beating fast. He is a tall man, taller than Shange, broad-shouldered with a big face. He smiled. I smiled back nervously. His hard expression that I had come to recognise over the past few days had disappeared. What is going on here? I thought.

'My brother will have a beautiful funeral,' he said.

'A beautiful funeral . . .?' I asked.

'Yes, you know the kinds of funerals they only have in towns.

My brother will have that type. It is confirmed. It will be a funeral such as this village has never seen before, with a coffin they will talk about for a long time.' He was excited.

'That is good,' I said when I noticed that Kauna was ignoring him.

'And the other thing is, Pastor Shoopala will conduct the funeral service. He said he wants to bury his "father" himself,' he said, his excitement increasing every minute.

Shange had named his last born after Pastor Shoopala and little 'Shopi' was his father's favourite. Shange was not much of a church-goer to receive all this attention.

'This is good to hear,' I said again. I wished Kauna would say something.

'Ya, it is really good. We are all happy.'

He must have been truly happy to come and share that piece of information with us, I thought. He stood there for a minute or so and left with a wide grin on his face.

'Did you hear that?' Kauna asked.

'Oh, you were listening? I thought you had gone temporarily deaf,' I snapped at her.

'I am sorry, Ali, it is just so hard to pretend. But these people have no shame. If it had been anyone else, anyone who had lived as Shange did, Pastor Shoopala would never ever have buried him,' Kauna continued bitterly. 'He would have used all manner of excuses not to allow his body in church. After all he was not a church-goer. He *never* asked for forgiveness. He never paid his tithes. He was abusive. He was a womaniser.'

'But they will never ever say that he was a womaniser.' I said. 'I'm pretty sure they mention all the sins of the dead, except that one. If, on the other hand, he had made financial contributions to the church, all his sins would be forgotten and his body would be allowed into the church and blessed. Mind you, his relatives will probably do that for him – pay, I mean,' I said,

141

thinking aloud. I could not imagine that Shange's family would ever allow one bad thing to be said about him, especially in church and at his funeral.

'I don't believe Pastor Shoopala would conduct the funeral service,' Kauna said reflectively, 'not unless he'd been paid. He is so two-faced. At least I think so. Do you remember what he did to the late old Nakawa's relatives?' Kauna reminded me.

'My dear, how can I forget?'

'First, he refused to have poor Nakawa's body enter the church to be blessed and then he gave the children a lecture! "You people only remember us when you're in trouble and when your loved ones die. We don't see your faces in church and some of you don't even greet us. When you are in your shining cars and wearing your expensive clothes, you think you are in heaven already," he lashed out at the children. Worse, he said she couldn't be buried among the "Christians" and should instead be buried outside the "Christian" cemetery. The children begged and pleaded, but he would not listen. He insisted that she died in sin because she was divorced and not forgiven. Soon after they buried their mother, the children left the village of Oshaantu. My heart went out to them. And now he is burying Shange. What happened to that whole "Christian" story? And to think Shange named my baby after Pastor Shoopala,' Kauna said, sounding annoyed.

'Aha, and do you know what they say about namesakes, "*Edhina Ekoogidho*".'*

'Don't remind me. They take right after their namesakes,' Kauna said, pulling a face as if dreading the idea that her son could take after Pastor Shoopala.

'By the way, doesn't it bother you that your in-laws have not consulted you about the funeral arrangements and the purchase

---

* 'They take right after their namesakes.'

of the coffin? I think that is extremely rude of them to go about as if you don't exist.'

'But I don't exist for them, except when they want me to do something, and I have too much to think about to worry about the colour of Shange's coffin.'

I had never known Kauna to be so clear, so firm. I was upset by the situation. I felt pulled this way and that, but there was something admirable in her behaviour, some new strength that I recognised, and it was surprisingly heart-warming.

Chapter Twelve

Mourners had just completed their morning prayer when my mother-in-law and I arrived at the mourning house. We greeted some of the people as we met them in the 'corridors' of the homestead. My mother-in-law joined a group of elderly women who were sitting in the corner of the main hut. I went to see Kauna.

As I bent down to pass through the door opening, I saw that her hut was full of people. I stood frozen in a bent position, not knowing whether to go in or retreat. 'Come in, dear, come in.' Mee Fennie rescued me from my uncertain position. My eye immediately caught the new face of a middle-aged man sitting on a trunk. I frowned lightly, wondering who he was.

Kauna's mother, Mee Maria, still holding her Bible and hymnal, sat on the bed with Mee Fennie and Kauna. Two other women sat at the foot of the bed. Kuku Peetu and another two women sat on the floor. It looked like a family gathering. To dispel the thought that I had intruded, Mee Fennie treated me like an old family friend; she stood up and offered me her space to sit down.

'Thank you, Mee Fennie, but I am fine here,' I said, pointing to the mud floor with my right hand. Kuku Peetu shifted his buttocks a couple of times to give me a bit more room. I was glad to be sitting next to him. He was quiet, even retiring, but I sensed that he had a wry view of certain conventions. I made myself comfortable then I exchanged greetings with each and everyone in the hut.

'You must be Mee Ali,' the voice from the trunk said. I turned to the middle-aged man. Now that my eyes had grown accustomed to the light, I could see who he was.

'Yes, Tate. And you must be Kauna's father,' I replied.

'This is my father, Tate Nambili,' Kauna said with such fondness that everyone looked at her. I greeted him again. He had a deep voice, a voice truly to fall in love with, it seemed to address you personally! It was so quiet in the hut that I began to wonder if it was because of my arrival.

'This is a big, well-built homestead,' Kauna's father remarked, looking at the thick poles and strong ropes that carried the thatched roof. He seemed genuinely impressed.

'Yes, father, this is a big compound,' Kauna agreed. 'Shange's relatives from Windhoek always get lost here.'

'I can believe it,' he replied. Again it fell quiet. I was about to leave when Kauna started to tell them about our encounter with Mee Kiito.

I wish Kauna had waited for me to leave, I thought, feeling uncomfortable. I did not really want to be part of the discussion, though I was curious to hear what Tate Nambili had to say. He remained silent, but looked intently at Kauna as she spoke, gently rubbing his hands together.

'You don't want to say goodbye words to your husband?' Kauna's mother asked, raising her voice.

We all looked at her. For a split second our eyes met. 'Why, *Ntowele*, why are you doing this?' she continued, lowering her voice. Kauna did not answer her mother.

Mee Fennie queried gently, 'Are you sure? I mean, are you quite, quite sure you don't want somebody to say a few words on your behalf, even goodbye words? All widows do this, you know.' It seemed she was still surprised by the decision that Kauna had taken.

'Yes, Mother, I am sure. Not even goodbye words,' Kauna

responded, looking across the room at each face in turn as if to assure them that she knew exactly what she was doing. 'I think this is best for me and Shange.'

I decided to excuse myself. I thought Mee Kiito would surely have told everybody that Kauna had refused to have something said on her behalf at her husband's funeral. However, despite my efforts to 'socialise' with those who were well known to be village gossips, nobody asked me anything about it!

It is said that 'You can't bury a man without attending his wake' and the mourning house was in commotion. People who had not found time to attend the wake during the course of the week came. Relatives and friends who could not leave their work earlier arrived, those who felt they did not attend the wake often enough were there, and those who were there every day were also present. The last day of the wake was the busiest of all during the mourning period. Final touches and arrangements for the burial day were being made. Friends, neighbours and relatives were still making contributions. They brought calabashes of *omalovu*, cases of beer and cool drinks, sheep and chicken. Meals and drinks had to be quadrupled. Close neighbours and friends assisted with cooking and feeding everybody. Mourners sat, stood or leaned against the homestead fence as they enjoyed their dinner. For some it was an opportunity to enjoy free alcohol. They did not miss a day. At times it was difficult to tell if they were mourning Shange or just wanted to get drunk.

All heads turned when Mukwankala arrived! I was pleasantly surprised to see her. I thought she would come for Kauna's sake. Since the incident with Shange at Mr Jackson's *cuca* shop more than two years previously, Mukwankala had not set foot in Shange's house. Conscious of the atmosphere she creates when she arrives at gathering places, she pretends she is not aware of curious looks. Like a queen accustomed to attention, she does not feel uncomfortable walking among a crowd. She sometimes greets and sometimes just nods at people she recognises. As usual she was neatly dressed. She wore her red *onyoka* necklace. She had applied *olukula* lotion to her face and arms, and its aroma filled the air as she passed each one of us. Her beautiful red *ontulo* dress was very colourful, with designs of flowers and butterflies. Supported by her stick, she took her time walking through all the mourners as if she were being given a standing ovation.

Mukwankala has the stature and grace of royalty. She reminds me of personalities in the many royal folk tales I have heard from my grandmother. Her friend, Mukwaanyoka, an elderly woman with whom she had come, pointed to a spot where they should sit. Still taking her time, she took a small mat from her brown bag and spread it on the ground. She made herself comfortable on the beautiful black and white mat of sheep's wool. Her friend followed suit.

Where in the world does she ever find enough water to look so fresh and clean? Water is in such scarce supply, I thought. Some say it is because she worked for many years for the missionaries as a domestic worker. But I think neatness is in her nature.

Once Mukwankala had been 'announced', she became the centre of attention. I went over to her as well, greeted her and thanked her for coming. I promised to inform Kauna of her presence. Mee Sofia also came over and greeted her. Mukwankala formally expressed her sympathy, then she and her friend were served with food and drinks of their choice. Mukwankala is well known for fearlessly speaking her mind. As a result she is popular among women, especially young women, and in no time women had gathered around her like bees around an exotic flower. Some joined her and stayed after they had made their greetings; others chatted for a little bit, but did not return to their seats. Two young women, Fiina and her friend Lucia, who made themselves comfortable next to Mukwankala, started to talk to each other.

'It must be very difficult to lose your husband these days,' Fiina said loud enough for Mukwankala to hear.

'Yes, you are right, Fiina. It is very difficult,' the other lady replied more loudly still.

'What is going to happen to poor Kauna?' another woman breast-feeding her baby interjected.

'Uuuh, I don't even want to think about it. Without a husband these days . . . hmmm?' Mee Fiina paused.

'Poor Kauna,' another woman said.

'Mmm, *mwa ti ko*,' Mukwankala finally began. 'I know one should not talk badly about the dead, but sometimes . . .' She shook her head. 'This Shange child really inherited his grandfather's bad hand.'

'He inherited a bad hand?' Fiina asked, fuelling Mukwankala's thought.

'Yes, a bad hand and a hot temper. Not the kind of man to marry anyone's daughter,' she said firmly, pulling her face in a definite *no*.

'He had a hot temper?' Fiina queried innocently.

'You don't know Shange. Where are you from?'

'Well, I . . . I . . .' Fiina mumbled, not sure what to say.

'We all remember how beautiful she was when she first arrived here as a new bride. Don't you remember?' Mukwankala asked. 'We called her the purple violet of Oshaantu. She was so delicate and she came when these flowers were in bloom.' The women nodded. 'Shange turned that child's beautiful face into something that looked as if it had been through some strange incisions made by a clan from outer space.' Mukwankala spoke her mind. 'Where have you seen a man chasing his wife who is running away from his claws into the neighbours' houses? Eh, tell me. Tell me, young woman, when have you ever seen anything like that?' Fiina wished she had returned to her seat earlier.

'How her parents ever allowed her to marry that bull goes beyond my understanding,' Mukwankala continued. 'How that poor child suffered. I don't think she had one happy day in her marriage. And then,' she said, as if she had remembered something else about Shange, 'he was like a pregnant woman, always moody and so unpredictable. I don't know why people would put up with a person like that! But he had friends.'

Mukwaanyoka, another elderly lady, poked Mukwankala with her right elbow. She had just finished eating a piece of meat and was busy cleaning her teeth with a piece of grass. Mukwankala quickly turned towards her.

'Ye, Mukwankala, *te ti . . . te ti . . .*,' she said, still cleaning her teeth.

'Ye, *Kaakandje*, I am listening,' Mukwankala encouraged her friend.

Mukwaanyoka spat out a morsel of meat before she continued. 'Tell me, I was just thinking . . . the child who died . . . Which one is it?' she asked in all seriousness and continued with her dental hygiene.

'Now, *Kaakandje*, what do you mean, "which child died"? Don't you know Shange?' Mukwankala asked, looking at her friend with an expression of irritation.

'All I know is that one of my childhood friends' children has died,' she answered with that I-know-what-I-am-talking-about attitude. 'I just don't know exactly which one. That woman had so many children.' Mukwaanyoka seemed oblivious to the surprised stares that greeted her question.

'So you don't know Shange? Shange ya Shange? The hot-hand boy we were just talking about with these women?' Mukwankala said, pointing at Fiina. Fiina wanted to hide.

'Well, I am only trying to remember whether he was the one who used to look after cattle with my first born, Shalli,' she said, narrowing her eyes as if trying very hard to remember the past.

'When was Shalli born?' Mukwankala asked.

'The year they destroyed the headman's fence.'

'So what year was that?'

'It is so long ago.'

'1930, 1940, . . . 50 . . . ?' Mukwaanyoka closed her eyes as if she were thinking very hard, then suddenly opened her eyes. 'During the reign of king Martin Kadhikwa, the year the missionaries built the second church down there,' she said, feeling pleased with herself for remembering. 'No, no, no! Shange was already a teenager by then . . .'

'Then he was my late Nakondja's age mate. He is the one who used to look after cattle with my late . . .'

'Yes, that is him . . .'

'*Yakwetu shili.*'* She cried so much it seemed as if she had heard the bad news for the first time. Mukwankala took her for a walk to comfort her.

◆

In another part of the homestead, where the mourning fire had been burning all week, stood a group of mostly young people. The atmosphere there was different. The mood was relaxed. Most of them were intoxicated with alcohol. They were cracking jokes, and laughter could be heard occasionally as they enjoyed their free meals and drinks to the full. As usual, Taleni, the clown of Oshaantu village, had come to entertain everyone. He was everybody's friend and relative. He never missed a

* 'Oh, poor thing.'

150

wedding or a funeral, but was always there to share in the grief or celebration. He spoke English well. People said that it was the English language that had made him crazy.

Taleni was standing so close to the fire that people feared he would fall into it, as he was not steady on his feet; and he was so thin that the slightest push would topple him over. Trying to get him away from the fire proved a rather risky business. He said what a bad husband Shange had been, 'But I will mourn him,' he reiterated over and over again. 'I will mourn him. Who is without mistakes? And who are we to pass judgement?' he asked, looking at people's faces as if he would find an answer there.

'The Gospel according to John, chapter eight verse seven in our Holy Bible says, "Whichever one of you has committed no sin may throw the first stone,"' he said. Then he bent down and broke off a piece of firewood and held it out to the mourners in an inviting manner. 'Well, then Jesus said, "I do not condemn you either. Go, but do not sin again."' People were impressed at how correctly he interpreted the Bible.

Chapter Thirteen

Kauna and I woke up to the voice of Mee Sofia and the smell of food. She stood in the middle of the hut, wearing black.

'Don't say you two women are still sleeping. Wake up! You have to get up and get ready.' She scolded us as if we were children who were very late for school. Kauna pulled the blanket over her head. I pulled it off. She stretched her body like a cat.

'Good morning, Mee Sofia,' I greeted her, ignoring her scolding.

'Good morning, Mee Ali. You must hurry.'

'Good morning, Mee Sofia.'

'Good morning, Mee Kauna. I can't believe you girls are still sleeping. What are you thinking about? As soon as you have finished eating, wash and get ready.' She put down a clay pot of beef stew and an *ontungwa* container with *oshithima* on the floor and left. 'Has she forgotten she is burying her husband today?' we heard Mee Sofia murmuring outside the hut.

'Who does she think she is?' Kauna asked.

'Your cousin-in-law,' I teased her.

'My cousin-in-law?' Kauna wrinkled her forehead. 'No wonder we overslept, it is chilly,' she said stretching herself again.

I climbed off the bed, peeped through the door opening and took a deep breath of fresh air. 'Hmmm . . . it looks as if it is going to rain.'

'Going to rain? For this one? I thought it only rained when good people had died,' Kauna remarked.

'Kauna ... Lower your voice. Besides, that is just a silly superstition. Get off the bed. Come wash your hands and let's eat.' We ate most of the food. I gave her one of the tablets Sustera had prescribed for her.

'Thank you again for agreeing to sleep over . . .'

'It's nothing.' I dismissed her gratitude with a gesture. 'Hush, I think someone is here,' I cautioned her.

One of Mee Sofia's daughters brought in a bucket of warm water. She told Kauna that the cousins from Windhoek would come and assist her to dress when she was ready.

Later, as Mee Sofia had said, Shange's relatives from Windhoek, mostly speaking a mixture of Oshiwambo and Otjiherero, came to help dress Kauna. They wrapped her up in black. Black skirt, black blouse, black sweater, black *sjalie*, black shoes, black pantihose and a black headscarf. Except for the handkerchief, which was white and decorated with colourful insect designs.

'Oto *munikwa nawa*,'* one of the Windhoekers remarked. Kauna didn't answer the compliment. She looked beautiful.

◆

Peep, peeeeeeeeeeeeeeeeeeeeeeeeeeeeeeeeeeeeeeeeeep. We heard the horns of the cars nearing the homestead. They had brought Shange home.

Customarily, all mourners had to leave the homestead to allow the coffin to enter the house. Only Kauna and I remained inside. The wailing outside increased. I felt overwhelmed by a sudden sadness. My nose burned and tears welled in my eyes. Kauna and I were quiet, each of us preoccupied with her own thoughts. They had removed a couple of sticks from the home-

* 'You look wonderful.'

153

stead fence to create a special portal for Shange, as the body was not allowed to pass through the same gate as the one he had used when he was alive. The special entrance was big enough to allow the six men carrying the coffin to pass through it and accompany Shange into his own house for the last time. Mee Sofia returned, her eyes red and swollen.

'Are you ready? We are waiting for you,' she said and added, 'to start with the prayer,' with that in-case-you-forgot-again expression on her face.

'Yes, yes, we are,' I said, looking at Kauna, who simply nodded. We walked slowly out of the hut. I led Kauna by her arm as we followed Mee Sofia through the large homestead to where the mourners had gathered, waiting for us. The air was heavy with collective sorrow. The homestead was packed with people who were there to accompany Shange in his last farewell to his house. People started to cry as soon as they saw Kauna. Many had not seen her since the death of her husband. Mee Sofia pointed at a chair, which had been prepared for her. I helped her to sit down. Kauna's parents and their delegations sat close by. Mourners watched her with confused glances and unspoken questions.

Shange's black and brown coffin rested on two benches about a metre away from Kauna.

Mee Maita was to facilitate the short ceremony. I hadn't seen her since the *okakungungu*, when I had softened towards her just a little. She stood up, holding a Bible and a hymn book. The wailing and crying softly diminished as the service was about to begin. I looked at Kauna and thought how deceptive was the colour black.

Mee Maita began, 'We are gathered here today to mourn the loss of our brother Shange . . .'

She knew the prayers and the rituals and, despite myself, I

was affected by her sense of occasion and the dignity she lent to this departure ceremony.

After she had concluded with the words, 'Go in peace and mourn because life is but short and but a vale of tears,' the mourners were given a chance to view Shange's body and the long mournful procession trickled out of the homestead.

Afterwards Mr Jackson and a few other men came forward, closed the coffin and carried it outside. Again Kauna and I waited until everybody had left, then Mee Sofia led us outside the house and informed us that Kauna and I would sit in a certain car.

'This side,' Salomo, Shange's older brother, instructed us, pointing to a shiny black car. I wondered what the car was for. 'Mee Ali and Mee Kauna should sit here at the back with mother, I will sit in front with the driver.'

We got into the car with the coffin behind us. There was a white man driving! Kauna and I watched him curiously. It was quite a car: beautiful cream curtains hung from the windows. I touched them gently.

There was a deafening silence as we drove slowly past the homesteads, *cuca* shops, school and clinic on our way to the church. There were about eleven cars following in the procession and the people in them continued to gossip. There were all kinds of rumours as to the cause of Shange's sudden death. His wife was, of course, number-one suspect followed by the ever 'jealous' neighbours.

'She got tired of his abuse and poisoned his breakfast.'

'She was jealous of his girlfriend and bewitched him.'

'She wanted to inherit his wealth and ate him up.'

'She wanted another man and killed this one.'

'Her parents on her mother's side are well-known witches. It runs in her clan.'

'First the neighbours got Shange fired from the mine and when they realised he still had money, they ate him up.'

It was about half past ten when we arrived at the church. The morning was still cloudy. There were many people waiting outside. People who chose not to go to the mourning house. The church was packed. There was not enough space for everybody. Some people sat outside, listening to the service through the doors and windows. They came from all over the country to bury Shange: former colleagues from the mine, relatives and friends from the cities, and people from Oshaantu village. They came from far and near. Many did not know the dead man personally, but they knew his relatives or friends or just somebody else who knew him.

Kauna, I and other close relatives sat in the front rows. Mee Kiito was indeed the mistress of the ceremony. The white man sat in the very last row, gnawing his fingernails throughout the service. I had never seen a white man attending a black funeral, let alone driving a funeral car! Later I was told that he was called a funeral undertaker. He came from Tsumeb. Apparently in town they do such things all the time; they let the white man bury their loved ones. It did not make sense to me. I couldn't help but think of what Salomo said, 'My brother will have a beautiful funeral, one such as nobody has seen in this village before.' There was a funeral programme and almost everybody got a copy. A passport-size photo of a much younger Shange appeared on the left-hand corner of the front page. Mr Jackson had obviously done a good job.

I scanned the programme and to my surprise noticed that a speaker was scheduled to speak on behalf of the widow. I panicked. Was there something I didn't know? Had they discussed the matter over the nights I had not slept at the mourning house? Had Kauna finally agreed to say something? What was going on? Slowly I looked around: to the left, to the right and again to the left, and then I poked Kauna with my right elbow. I slowly raised the programme to eye-level and with my index finger pointed to where it was typed, 'On behalf of the widow'. We communicated with our eyes. She knew nothing about the widow's speech. What was Mee Kiito up to? I thought, worried. Pretending that she was fixing her *sjalie*, covering part of her face, Kauna gave me a 'don't worry' sign, with her left hand.

Don't worry, don't worry? Is she crazy? I thought. Yes, she is crazy. This woman is crazy. I have known it since the day Shange died. Kauna has lost it, I thought, unhappy and frustrated. Who will deliver the speech? Me? Yes, they will look at me. Everybody will expect me to say something on behalf of the widow. Yes, but what? What will I say? What? I can say something. I can . . . I started to rehearse my speech silently.

Dear mourners, I am standing here on behalf of the widow, Mee Kauna. No no, that is no way to start a widow's speech.

Mee Kauna is also my 'daughter', as my only daughter is named after her beloved husband Tate Shange. Kauna will never let me say that!

I am saying these words as if they come right from Mee Kauna's own mouth. No. This doesn't sound right.

I am standing here to pay Kauna's last tribute to her husband and the father of her five children. She is deeply shocked, no numbed, by the sudden death of Shange. Would she allow that?

It is very hard for the children to lose a loved one, particularly a father. Must I say something about the children?

They got married fourteen years ago and have five children, three girls and two boys. They will miss the peace and happiness in their home. Kauna will kill me.

He was such a generous person. That feels easy to say.

Rest in peace.

I was frantically trying to remember all the many phrases

uttered on behalf of widows that I had heard at their husbands'
funerals. But none of the phrases felt right. God, help me, I
thought. I felt sweat on my forehead. It was so hot and stuffy
in the church. I took the programme and used it as a fan to
cool my face. It was a long programme and many speakers
were scheduled to speak.

Omuwiliki gwoshituthi	Mee Kiito
Funeral service	Pastor Shoopala
Welcoming remarks	Tate Lukasa
On behalf of Shange's clan	Tate Salomo
On behalf of the widow	
On behalf of the widow's clan	Mee Fennie Nangolo
On behalf of the neighbours	Tate Shuuya
On behalf of the friends	Mr Jackson
On behalf of the colleagues	Rickie

Pastor Shoopala, Pastor Hallao, Tate Mbenjameni and Mee
Maita appeared through the door that led to the altar. The
congregation stopped singing and stood up to acknowledge
their presence. Pastor Shoopala started the service standing in
front of the coffin, which rested on the altar floor with a big
wreath on top of it.

'I am the resurrection and the life, whoever believes in me
shall live even if he is dead.'

As Pastor Shoopala conducted the service, a local photogra-
pher started to take pictures from all corners of the altar. At
one point Pastor Shoopala stopped and gave him a disapproving look. The pastor performed his duties between songs and
speeches, then at last it was the widow's speech. My heart
raced, my throat felt dry. There was a heavy silence in church.
I looked at the woman sitting next to me, sitting there as if

nothing was happening. Not giving a damn in the least. Sha! I thought, angrily. Where did she get this strength from anyway?

'On behalf of the widow please,' Mee Kiito called for a second time. 'Is there a speaker for the widow?' she asked, acting as if she were confused.

People started to whisper. I couldn't just sit there. I decided to stand up, but I couldn't. I should, but I couldn't. I looked at Kauna again. She was staring straight ahead, blinking her eyes as if she were trying to get used to the light. Finally, bravely, I decided to stand, when I heard something at the back.

'Uuuhhh!' people called out. I turned my head to see what had caused the loud murmur and I was just in time to see Kauna's uncle, kuku Peetu, strolling up to the altar.

'Thank you very much,' Mee Kiito said to kuku Peetu and looked in our direction with a pleased expression on her face. Kauna sat quietly, her head bowed, staring at her hands.

Kuku Peetu, tall and slender, in his navy-blue wrinkled blazer, pink shirt and yellow pants, stood at the altar and courageously faced the congregation. He had black spots round his eyes that looked like damage from skin-lightening chemicals; his hair appeared as if it had been combed with a hot brush. Standing up at the front of the church, he looked oddly vulnerable. Would people think he was ridiculous? But then, I thought, he has always had a sense of occasion, and I didn't feel quite so anxious.

'On behalf of the widow, Mee Kauna, and we the relatives of the widow . . .' he began his speech, one written nowhere, in a voice so low that it sounded as if he were speaking out of real distress. 'I would like to express the deepest sadness at the death of Tate Shange. Firstly as son-in-law, brother, son, father and husband,' he said and he sounded genuinely sad. 'I speak for the Nambili family and particularly for the widow here,' he went on and bent his head in our direction. I looked at Kauna expecting to see her angry or irritated, but she was smiling! Did she know something I didn't, or was it just that kuku Peetu could do no wrong, because he had always been kind to her?

'We have been delivered a severe blow by Shange's death,' kuku Peetu continued, just as if he were close to tears. I couldn't help but begin to feel amused as well. If it was an act, he was performing like a star!

'He was such a good man, a caring husband and always ready to help . . .' His voice started to fade. He reached into the pockets of his yellow pants and pulled out a lime-green hand-kerchief, wiped his eyes, blew his nose and continued the widow's speech. Kauna looked at me. I decided not to look at her, while kuku Peetu continued for a bit in the same way. I thought we both might just laugh out loud.

'The Nambili family did not only lose a son-in-law, but also a pillar of strength,' he concluded.

I was amazed at his confidence. To stand there, in front of people he didn't know and not only talk with such ease, but openly show emotion. Wiping a final tear from his eyes, he left the altar and drifted back down the aisle. Some people smiled at him as he passed by.

As the ceremony progressed it grew hotter and hotter in the church and more people began to use the programmes as fans to cool themselves down. It was long after midday and there were still many speakers and choirs who had not spoken or sung. We are going to be here until sunset, I thought, feeling tired, and my mind drifted off. Now and then I heard speakers almost repeating each other. 'He was such and such and such a good man.' I snorted at some of the euphemisms. How could people be such hypocrites? Occasionally I looked at Kauna to observe her reactions, but most of the time she sat there showing no emotion at all. I sighed deeply.

'In the interest of time we will have to cut certain things short,' Mee Kiito announced at last. 'All remaining choirs should prepare one song each please and the remaining speakers will be given just five minutes each.'

I heaved a sigh of relief when the programme finally ended. Pastor Shoopala was just about to conclude the service when Tate Mbenjameni, who was not scheduled to speak, asked to say 'only a few words'. I could have died! Why do people enjoy talking so much? I thought, feeling like yelling. He begged the relatives of the deceased not to trouble the widow and the children.

'It is our custom that we inherit things from our loved ones when they pass away. I believe we do this to treasure their memories, but I want to remind the relatives of the deceased who are here today, that when they do so, they should please think of the wife and the children, particularly the children's education.' He thanked everybody who came to bury Shange, especially those who had travelled long distances, and wished them a safe journey back home.

I was happy he had spoken. I hoped they would not bother Kauna and the children. Maybe now they would, at least, think twice before they did so.

'We have come to the end of the second phase of this ceremony. Now we need to move to the cemetery,' Mee Kiito announced. 'Those who wish to view Shange's body may do so as we leave.'

Everyone stood up. Meme Kiito suggested a song. The top half of the coffin was opened to reveal Shange's face, so that people could look at him as they passed by. The mourners moved row by row, filed up to the coffin and viewed the dead man's face. Some stopped and made pious gestures to demonstrate their respect, others touched his face, a few bent their knees or bowed their heads. Some wept all over again.

Kauna, I and the closest family members were the last to leave the church. I followed Kauna to the coffin. Strange, but Shange looked as if he were just sleeping and might sit upright at any time. I accelerated my pace.

It was so good to be outside again, there was so much fresh air. I inhaled the cool breeze as deeply as I could. The sky was still cloudy and it looked as if it might rain.

'Kuku Peetu talked rubbish,' Kauna whispered.

'Ya, he did,' I whispered back.

As for me, it did not matter whether kuku Peetu talked rubbish or not. I was just happy someone had spoken on behalf of the widow.

At the cemetery, I had to stay close to Kauna. The older women advised it, in case she collapsed and needed my support to keep her from falling. I did stand beside her, but it was to protect her from the eyes of the very same people. Everyone was staring at her curiously. 'Maybe at the funeral she will cry,' some gossiped. Still nothing happened. Even the sight of her children did not make her emotional. At times I felt like hiding her face.

Mourners formed a circle around Shange's grave. Almost everyone wore black; most men wore dark sunglasses. As we sang, the white man came forward to put the coffin away. He brought a green carpet and laid it on the grave. The men around came forward to assist. They brought four silver irons and put them on top of the green carpet. We watched the men as they hooked the coffin on rubber-like strings attached to the four silver irons. A green-carpet funeral, I thought. We watched as the coffin was slowly lowered into the ground. Mourners, especially relatives, began to cry. They called Shange's name out loud. Shange's baby sister, affectionately known as 'Nkelo', almost threw herself into the grave. One of the men quickly held her back. 'They were close,' some remarked.

As the coffin was being lowered, the woman from the white house cried like a hungry hyena. It made me uncomfortable. She made everyone cry all over again. Friends and relatives held her up as if she could not stand on her own. Her arms and body hung loose. Her pregnancy was clearly visible. They put her on the ground and patted her forehead with a wet cloth. She leaned against a relative. She too was wrapped in black. I wondered if the Windhoek people had anything to do with the clothes. For a few minutes she was the centre of attention. Those who felt strong enough kept on singing until the coffin touched the ground. The nurse said that he had had a heart attack.

Pastor Shoopala came forward, the wind gently blowing the edges of his massive dress. 'Dust to dust,' he read.

As was the custom, the men, ready with their shovels, came forward and dipped them into the sand. Then the closest relatives moved forward, took sand from one of the full shovels and released it over the coffin. Kauna did likewise. I assisted the children to do the same. Relatives and friends followed. People started to go round and round the grave, taking sand from the shovels and sprinkling it over the coffin.

Then the men took turns to shovel sand onto the grave. For a while everything fell quiet, but for the sound of the damp sand leaving the shovels and a hollow resounding thud as it fell on the eternal wood, which awaits us all. Shovelful by shovelful. The men were at work. Finally the grave was covered. A big wreath was placed on top of the mound. Under this earth lies Shange, I thought. It was all over.

Small talk began to filter through the air and even laughter could be heard. People used the opportunity to visit the graves of their friends and loved ones. Some graves were sadly neglected and clearly forgotten. Maybe because the dead were no longer consulted. Only a few graves were well kept. The procession back to the mourning house was not as quiet and orderly as when it had arrived. People moved from group to group, meeting friends and exchanging greetings. 'Truly, he is buried,' one of the mourners remarked.

Kauna, I and other relatives were among the last to leave the cemetery. We climbed into the long shiny black car and drove home. I turned around and looked at Shange's grave. It became smaller and smaller with every metre we left behind us. 'Wait, stop the car, we can't leave Shange alone there!' I felt like screaming.

As soon as we arrived back at the homestead, Shange's relatives started to serve people with food and drinks. It was a feast. A number of cattle were slaughtered in Shange's honour. The death of a wealthy man often feeds the whole village.

Later, as I walked home with my mother-in-law, I looked at the sky. The stars were coming out. Would Shange be among them?

Chapter Fourteen

On Sunday, mourners from Windhoek and colleagues from the mine left first thing in the morning. They had a long way to travel. Kauna's father and all her family, except her mother and aunt, as well as some of Shange's relatives, left later in the day. I decided to go to church.

'I thought you didn't like going to church by yourself,' said my daughter, looking rather surprised.

'What makes you think that? Of course I like going to church . . .' I stumbled over my own words.

'I've only seen my *mbushe* going to church alone,' she giggled.

Kids! I thought.

After church I stayed at home and watched the commotion at the Shanges'.

Three days after Shange's burial, Kauna's mother and aunt met with the most important members of the Shange family to talk about the future of Kauna, her children and the homestead.

'Well, here is our daughter, she is still young . . . We have given her to you . . .,' Kauna's mother said.

What was she suggesting? Kauna was shocked.

'I definitely don't think we should discuss this now,' replied Mee Fennie, aware of her sister's intentions and dismissing them.

'Kauna is our daughter and she can stay here if she wants to. She is the mother of our nieces, nephews and grandchildren,' the great uncle Sheya said, putting little Shopi on his lap and stroking his head. Kauna's mothers left with the understanding that their daughter could stay where she was.

It did not look as if the extended Shange family was going to leave the homestead quickly. As a result I did not see Kauna as often as I wanted to. When I visited her, I did not stay long. The atmosphere was so cold, and I felt their hostility towards Kauna. One of Shange's cousins moved into their nuptial bedroom. Kauna was still staying in the hut. I had to get used to the idea of my friend wearing nothing but black.

A month after Shange's death, Kauna received a visit from the headman. He explained the whole process of compensation for the homestead. He told her that since the owner who had paid for it had died, she should now pay for it, if she intended to stay on and become the new owner. Kauna discussed the matter with her in-laws. They agreed with the headman; it was the custom. Kauna informed them that she was familiar with the custom and she would honour the headman's request. However, she needed time to raise all the money that was needed.

A week later Kauna received a message from the headman. He informed her that her in-laws had paid for the homestead and were now the new owners. Her destiny was now in their hands.

'Why do you want to stay here and enjoy Shange's wealth? You didn't even shed one tear for him. Do you think we don't know how you disrespected Shange? Now you want to stay here and behave like a poor widow. You will not stay here and bring other men into Shange's bed. If you think we would allow this, we won't,' they told her.

◆

'They have asked me to leave . . .'
    'What?' I asked.

'Ya, they did. Why am I crying? I expected this.'

'I thought they said you could stay?'

'Ag, you did not believe that, did you?'

'Listen, these days they cannot make you leave the homestead. I wanted to tell you about this. I have heard about organisations at Ongwediva and Oshakati that support widows with problems like yours. Surely they will not allow your in-laws to take away the homestead from you and the children,' I said, hopefully.

'How could they possibly stop it?' she asked, disbelieving.

'Well, I think they . . . they will bring lawyers and police and . . .'

'No, no, Ali,' she replied dismissively, shaking her head. 'I don't want to fight with these people. I just wish they had told me earlier. I will leave, no problem.'

'And the children?'

'This is my baggage and your own baggage is never too heavy to carry. I am taking them with me.'

Chapter Fifteen

I cooked a goodbye dinner for Kauna. I slaughtered a chicken and cooked *evanda*. She loved chicken and the *evanda* was for good luck and a safe journey. I brewed *omalovu* too, but that was more for me than for her. We sat at Michael's *oshinyanga* and had our dinner there.

'I will miss you, Ali. I will never forget you. You will always be part of me, always,' Kauna said suddenly.

'Oh, Kauna, I will miss you too.' I felt a lump in my throat. 'I'm sad that you are leaving but I know you can't stay.'

I was sipping my second *oshitenga* when Kauna said, 'I need to confess something to you. I have thought about doing this for the past few years, and whether I should tell you or not. Now I'm convinced that I should tell you before I leave. However, you must first promise me that you will not be angry with me.'

'What do you need to confess?' I could not imagine what to expect.

'Promise me first,' she said.

'I promise.'

'I once wronged you and I need to get it off my chest . . .'

'I can't imagine that you have wronged me,' I interrupted. 'And if you did, I'm sure it was not intentional. So please drop the idea, if you are going to make a confession. We need to spend this evening partying and planning how the two of us can visit each other as often as possible.'

Kauna took no notice. 'Of course it is not something that I've done or said; it is rather what I wished for you.' I felt uneasy; I did not want anything to spoil the evening.

'Please, don't look so worried. It's probably not so dreadful.' She laughed a little to lighten the atmosphere.

I was afraid. I hoped she would not say anything that would cruelly unmask me and destroy our friendship, which had not always been sugar-sweet. There had been tensions that had resulted in our not visiting each other, arguments about children, and other small things that had come between us, but nothing more – nothing serious that might warrant 'a confession'.

'Well, this is the story. I was jealous. I was jealous of you. I was jealous of your marriage. I was jealous of your children, I was jealous of the manner in which you and Michael interacted.' She scrutinized my face while she was talking. She was talking a little too fast. 'Your marriage is so beautiful, Ali. It is too good to be true. Nothing ever seems to go wrong. The manner in which your husband conducts himself and treats everybody else makes him feared and respected. He is so dignified. He is not like one of those men who get drunk at *cuca* shops and disgrace themselves and their loved ones. People have said he is not a "real" man, because he does not sleep around, does not get drunk and silly, and does not neglect his children. I have been waiting for the day when he would get tired and decide to prove that he too was a "real" man. But that day has never come and now I believe it will never will. I love that about him. I love his uncompromising attitude to right and wrong. I would give anything to have a husband like Michael,' she said emphatically. She examined her hand as if she were looking for a scratch. There was a long pause. 'But then, without warning, one day I woke up with this terrible anger. I don't remember being so angry in my entire life. Shange was not even home, he was at the mine, so I don't know what caused this mood,' she said, as if she still did not understand.

'I was full of hatred and resentment with the whole world. With my marriage, my children, my relatives, this village and with God, but particularly with you.'

'With me?' I was shocked. She looked at her hands again, spreading her fingers wide.

'Yes, with you,' she said and looked away. 'I felt that God had been unfair to me.' She moved and the moon caught her face, revealing an expression that I didn't recognise immediately.

'So how was God unfair and why did you hate and resent me?' I felt hurt. I had not done anything. I had always tried to support Kauna, though the memory of the photograph flashed through my mind. I had not meant to upset her, but I had upset her.

'Look. I was the child of a pastor, well brought up, obedient to my parents and elders. I did not sleep around, my husband was the first man I had ever slept with. I thought why? Why me? What have I done to God to have a husband like mine? That day I prayed that something bad would happen to you or to Michael. I actually wished you harm. Michael could have married any woman he wanted to, but he chose you.'

I felt my body go cold.

'Kauna, what are you saying?' I whispered, not sure if my question was loud enough for her to hear me.

'Yes, Ali, I wished you harm. But that awful mood did not last long,' she added quickly. 'I was shocked by that side of myself. I was afraid of my own thoughts. For some time I could not look at my face in the mirror. I didn't believe I was capable of such thoughts. I felt so bad that I could possibly have wished you harm. You of all people, can you imagine?' she asked, her eyes examining my face. I looked at her not knowing what to

170

say. 'You, the one and only good thing that has ever happened to me in this village. Can you believe it?' she asked, laughing almost hysterically.

'That thing made me so moody, I even slapped Kandiwapa, my Kandiwapa,' she said, shaking her head slowly. 'Wonderful as you always are, you probably thought I was pregnant. When I came to my senses, it was too late. Your husband had been in that terrible minibus accident. I thought I would go crazy. I panicked, I prayed. I begged for God's mercy and forgiveness. I prayed for Michael's life, day and night. "God, if I cannot have a good marriage, let me have this one thing, Ali's friendship. Save her husband," I prayed. Michael was the only man in this village who ran to my rescue when my husband beat me. How could I have ever wished him harm? I made a promise to God that if he saved Michael's life, I would never ever wish ill on anybody, not even my husband, for as long as I live.'

I remembered how Kauna insisted that I take as long as I needed to care for Michael in the hospital; that I should not worry about my children and mother-in-law while I was away. She made sure they were fed well and taken care of. She even worked in our field! I thought she was doing what I would have done for her if she had been in my situation.

'This feeling was hard for me. I could not sleep. My best friend, I hope you can find it in your heart to forgive me. I will never do anything to hurt you, believe me,' she pleaded. I didn't know what to say. She looked at me waiting for a response.

'Believe me,' she urged again.

'I believe you,' I said rather coldly. 'So you thought life was unfair because I, whore and slut who should have married Shange, got married to Saint Michael, and you, Virgin Mary, thought it was my fault.'

'Oh no, Ali . . .'

'I must say I am quite disappointed that you of all people

could also think this of me. Let me tell you, Kauna, I did not get married a virgin, but I certainly did not sleep around.'

'Oh, Ali, I never meant it that way . . .' The tears that she had been trying to contain poured down her face. She fell on her knees and cried uncontrollably.

'Please, Kauna, I'm sorry, don't cry. Please stand up. It is nothing. Really, nothing.' I pulled her up. 'Well, it is nice to see you crying,' I said and she laughed and cried and laughed and cried.

'Kauna, please know this. Michael is a good man, but this has nothing to do with me. I wanted a good man. I prayed for one; I think I just got more than I asked for. Shange was the man he was and again it had nothing to do with you. Don't take it personally. He would have treated any woman he married in the same way.'

'But not you, Ali, not you,' she said, shaking her head.

'Well, he would have treated me like that too, but just not for so long.'

'You would have left him?'

'Oh yes. I want to be a wife, not a punching bag. When Michael and I got married, his relatives complained that he was marrying a woman whose mother was divorced and apparently that was a bad omen. But here we are still married and we will be married for the rest of our lives.' Kauna sighed. 'Come on, don't worry now. It's over. Let's forget all about this now, or do you have anything else to confess?' I asked her lightly.

She shook her head, smiling. I smiled too.

'As a child I used to wonder what was in there. I was almost obsessed,' I said, looking at the full moon.

'And now?' Kauna asked.

'I guess I have lost that sense of wonder.'

Chapter Sixteen

Kauna got rid of most of her belongings. She gave two goats, a male and a female, to my daughter as presents.

'When I see you again, you should have a whole *kraal*, full of goats.'

'Oh yes, yes, Mee Mbushe,' my daughter said, excited.

The rest Kauna slaughtered. She distributed most of her baskets and clay pots among the women, some of whom she had befriended since the *okakungungu* day. Some of her valuables, like her three *oonyoka* necklaces, she gave to Sustera, Mukwankala and me.

'You are giving everything away,' I complained.

'No, these things need to go,' she said.

On the day she prepared to leave Oshaantu, Mukwankala came by early in the morning to bid her farewell. She put oil on her head and wished her good luck.

The Shange family observed everything from the sidelines, making critical remarks and gossiping. They had 'won' in that they had the homestead, but it was not a moral victory, and they seemed to be aware of this, which made them more bitter and angry.

So, when the time came for Kauna to go, it was again my daughter and I who accompanied my friend and her children to the main road to catch a lift. I tried not to cry. I tried to be strong for my friend Kauna and her family.

They looked like people who were going away for a weekend, they had so little luggage. Each one of them was able to carry their own personal belongings, and Kauna held Shopi's hand.

'I guess you are saying, "shoo", never ever will I have anything to do with men of that generation again.'

'Me?' she asked, pointing at herself. 'No. No, I don't think so. You have not seen anything yet. You know what happens to the *mahangu* millet? After it has been knocked down, stepped on and mercilessly destroyed by cattle, it finds the strength to repair itself and grow better. It is often bigger and more vibrant than the millet that has not been threatened by any danger and cut to the ground,' she said. 'No, I am not finished with them, I am only just starting.' She shook her head slowly as if she were giving this idea long and careful thought.

'Yes, you are right!' I said, excited. 'But with whom will I fetch water and wood, with whom will I go to church, gossip and attend all those social gatherings?'

'You will find somebody,' she assured me.

'You are moving so far away, will I ever see you?'

'*Kuna mukweni ha kokule*,'* she said, hopeful.

'Absolutely. Where your heart is, there is your treasure,' I echoed her sentiment. I looked at her and wondered, if she had 'confessed' to me earlier, would it have affected our friendship?

'Have you forgiven me?'

'Yes, I have,' I said, almost blushing.

'I love you.'

'I love you too.'

Kauna looked at the dusty gravel road ahead of us and said, 'I don't know what is out there for me and my children, but I will go, I am willing.'

---

* 'It is never far away where a relative resides.'

174

Chapter Seventeen

Michael came home five weeks after we had buried Shange for the primary reason of expressing his sympathy to the Shange family. He arrived at about 2 a.m. on Saturday morning. I had never been so happy to see my husband. I literally threw myself into his arms and cried and cried. 'It's OK, it's OK,' he kept saying in a comforting way. I don't know why I cried so much, but I wept as if my heart would break. When the kids woke up they were happily surprised by the presence of their father. Saturday morning was never that jubilant in our homestead. With the promise that he would be home by lunchtime, he left to greet the Shanges.

Michael apologised for not attending the funeral of his childhood friend. 'This is the earliest I could come and I am only here till tomorrow.'

'Everything went well. The support was enormous. Neighbours, friends and relatives extended their help. I thank God that He guided all. Mourners came and returned safely,' Shange's mother told him. 'No, Shange was buried, truly buried,' she said with a sense of pride and visible pain.

'Here is something to wipe your tears,' Michael said and handed her a beautiful reddish material with which to make a traditional *ontulo* dress. Michael, accompanied by Mee Sofia, went to Shange's grave. He took a handful of sand and sprinkled it over the mound. He then gently stroked the plate on the cross where Shange's name was engraved.

Oh my friend, Makula, friend from my childhood, Giant of

Oshaantu, you have stretched forever. Silenced forever, I will miss you, always . . ., Michael thought as he stroked the plate gently.

From the cemetery, Michael went to greet neighbours from the homesteads nearby. When he arrived home it was towards sunset. I complained bitterly.

'You cannot greet the whole village.'

'I couldn't just pass them by like that, they will feel offended.'

'They should understand that you are only here for the weekend and you promised the kids that you would be here by lunchtime.'

'I know, I know, but you know what people are like . . .'

The children and I had slaughtered a goat while he was on his village-greeting mission. We cooked his favourite dishes, *oshithima* with goat stew, roasted goat, caterpillars. The boys roasted the meat. They were so excited. It was not every day that they were treated to so much meat. My daughter and I did the stew and brewed *omalovu*. The sun had already gone down when Michael finally found the time to sit with us. He was pleasantly surprised by our efforts to prepare a small feast for him. It was a rare occasion when Michael, my mother-in-law, the children and I all sat around the fire enjoying our dinner together. As usual, the children were all over their father, competing for his attention. Each one had something to tell or show him. Thomasa showed him a drum that he had made himself.

'I made it, Daddy,' he told his father proudly and beamed when Michael beat the drum a few times.

Pandu, who comes after Thomasa, ran to his hut and returned with a car made of silver wire to show his father. 'I also made this for myself,' he said, holding on to his short pants that are so torn they look more like a skirt and keep falling down.

'What kind of car is this?' his father asked.

'It's a Ford.' Michael made a few car sounds. Pandu beamed with joy. Michael turned to Kauna.

'And you, my only princess, what do you have to show me?' Kauna rubbed her back against the fence of the *oshinyanga* before she responded.

'I passed this term's examination.'

'Wonderful,' Michael called out, genuinely happy.

'What about you, *mbushe*? You seem so quiet.'

'Nothing,' Michael junior said, more to himself than to his father. He held a stick to the fire, separating the hot coals from the wood.

'Don't worry. Next time,' Michael said and rubbed his head.

Then Kangulu, the little gossip, started to tell on me, informing his father how I beat them for nothing and didn't always give them the goodies he sent us.

'Mother gives everything you send us to other people, especially Kandiwapa's mother.' I gave him a severe look that he chose to ignore. Grandmother was not spared. 'Kuku doesn't like us to listen to the radio,' continued Kangulu. 'She says, "It's for the news bulletin and the calling-in programme." We don't even listen to the children's stories and songs any more. She says the radio battery will run out.'

'We listen to the songs on Sundays,' Thomasa said.

'Yes, only on Sundays,' conceded Kangulu, changing his story. 'Maybe you should buy us our own radio, Tate.' The little boy revealed his hand.

'Yes, maybe I should buy you your own radio.'

'Daddy, Daddy, do you know what? The song you taught us to sing for the cattle whenever we want them to return home, it works! It's unbelievable! It's like they understand the song. As soon as we start to sing, they all start walking home. Did you used to sing for the cattle too, Daddy, when you were big like me?'

'Yes, I used to do that. I used to sing for my father's cattle too.'

To everybody's amusement, Kangulu stood up and started to sing the song.

> '*Eengobe dange noyikombo yange*
> *tu endeni tuye keumbo*
> *latoka nale nomulaulu*
> *wa hala ku tu tilifa . . .*'*

Michael clapped his hands for him. 'You should be a musician when you grow up,' he said.

'Yes, yes,' Kangulu replied, excited, wanting to sing for us again.

'No, no, *opuwo*, it's enough,' Thomasa ordered Kangulu. 'Besides, I am the one who started to talk about the song.'

'Daddy, the brown cow had a calf and the mother died,' Thomasa informed his father.

'Really, what happened?'

'And he cried the whole day, hiii . . . hiii . . . hiii,' Kangulu interrupted, to Thomasa's embarrassment.

'You have such a big mouth,' Thomasa snapped at his brother.

'Don't talk to your brother like that.'

'Daddy, he always . . .'

'It is OK, Son. And you have to watch your mouth,' Michael warned Kangulu.

It was time for the presents, which diverted some attention away from Michael. Everybody got something – a pair of shoes, pants, a dress, material or perfume.

---

* Cattle of mine,
Goats of mine,
Let's move towards home,
It's already late, and darkness wants to frighten us.

My mother-in-law was first to announce that she was going to bed and she was followed by Michael junior. One by one they all departed. Finally we were alone.

'Next time I will stay for longer,' he said. I just nodded, looking away.

'Is it just my imagination or is my namesake rather quiet?' I told him about the Ngonyofi incident at school. He listened but did not respond immediately.

'I will talk to him in the morning, before I leave. Next time I will visit for longer,' he repeated. 'I hear the funeral went well,' he said, after a while.

It was more of a question than a statement. So I told him everything from the moment of Shange's death to the burial. He listened without comment, but his face revealed his feelings as he watched me speaking.

'How did you handle Kauna's departure?' he asked with real interest. I love this man!

'Oh, it was very hard, we cried . . ., I cried,' I said shyly. He smiled at me. 'I miss her. I was so used to having her around, I will expect her to come knocking for a long time.'

'What about new friends?'

'I feel as if their eyes are saying, "Are you going to befriend us now that Kauna is gone?"'

'What about Sustera?'

Yes, Sustera, why not? She is a good person, who will always wish you well, I thought.

I told him about Kauna's confession. I couldn't tell if he was amused or shocked. He was so quiet, I thought he would not say anything at all. Finally he spoke.

'Kauna saw what she had done. She saw how unhappiness and jealousy could be so destructive. I admire her for telling you. I have seen how relatives and friends destroyed the marriage of Jacopo,' he continued. Michael does not often talk

179

about his old friend, but when he does, it is with affection. I remembered the story.

'That's funny,' I said. 'I was thinking about Jacopo and Mee Nangula just a few days ago. I was thinking about them because it seems that loyalty to one's family must always come before loyalty to one's in-laws.'

'Yes,' answered Michael. 'I think that is in our tradition, but so much is changing now and we are not changing with it fast enough. If Mee Nangula had not been such a good business-woman who managed so well on her own, Jacopo's relatives would not have been so jealous.

'But, remember, I told you that I'd learned something through all that whole saga and I was determined not to make the same mistake. I promised myself that I would not allow any family member or friend to ruin my marriage. With God's help, I will handle my marriage myself,' he said.

You have never told me all this, I thought, but deep down I somehow knew that this was what made Michael different.

It seemed surprising that Shange had to die before I understood what Michael thought about marriage and relationships, or at least before he told me so directly. I was tempted to ask him to leave his work in Windhoek to come and live with us and find a job in the government.

'Michael, I don't always say this, but I want to thank you for what you do for us . . . I appreciate it, even though I miss you and it is not always so easy to bring up the children by myself,' I said, smiling shyly. It felt difficult to say, but I continued. 'I know of husbands who work on mines and farms and find themselves other wives and simply never return home. But you always come back to us.' He looked at me quietly.

'Thank you,' he said after a bit. There was a twinkle in his eyes. 'What is all this about? Does it have anything to do with Shange's death? Is it Kauna's confession?' he asked, smiling.

'No, what are you talking about?' I replied innocently.

'Well, all the goat slaughtering and brewing of *omalovu*, all this feasting tonight, and the way you have treated me since I arrived this morning, the way you looked at me, and now you are thanking me for being a good father and a husband.'

'The way I looked at you . . .'

'Yes, not that I don't like what you say, in fact it is good to know, it feels good indeed. It is just you have never said so much in all the eleven years of our marriage.'

'But you love goat meat and I . . .' I shrugged my shoulders, not sure what to say and feeling embarrassed at the same time.

'I don't disagree with you, it's just, it seems different . . . you seem to be being extra nice to me this time,' he said and patted me on the shoulder. He stood up and reached for the *oshin-yanga* fence for support. It was pitch dark. There was only the fading fire and the sounds of the insects in the darkenss.

'Let's go to bed,' he said. 'It is after midnight already. I have to wake early if I want to catch the early morning bus.' He stretched his hand out to me. I held onto it as I stood up. He put his arms around my waist and felt the beads around it, which sent a thrill through my body.

'Yes, let's go to bed,' I answered.

Glossary

This glossary contains words from Oshiwambo, one of the many languages used in Namibia, together with a few words from Afrikaans, which is still widely used there.

Aakuusinda   a clan, literally 'clan of snakes'
bakkie   (Afrikaans) small pick-up truck
cuca shop   rural store that sells general goods and alcohol
ee   yes
eewa   OK
egumbo   house
elilo   traditional plate
epya   plot, land for cultivation
etemo   hoe
evanda   spinach, pounded and dried
iitenga   wooden cup
Ila, ila   Come here, come here
kaakandje   my friend
kafau   traditional home-brewed beer
kangala   violet
kraal   (Afrikaans) pen in which cattle are kept
kuku   grandmother, grandfather
mahangu   millet
marula   wild plum tree
mbushe   namesake
meme   mother, aunt
mememweno   mother-in-law

mevrou   (Afrikaans) madam, teacher

miitiri   teacher

mutakati   medicine

muti   medicine

mwa ti ko   say what!

nakusa   the deceased

ne   you (plural/honorific)

nganga   traditional healer, herbalist 'witchdoctor'

ntowele   second-born child (affectionate way of addressing a child)

nyee nyee nyee   person who talks rubbish

okakungungu   working festival, group cultivation

okatokele   home-brew, home-made alcohol

olukula   reddish lotion, traditional herbal cream/powder used on the skin

omahangu   millet

omalovu   home-brew

omatala   flea-market

omatemba   wooden plate

omatemos   hoes; plural of *etemo*

ombili   pardon, peace

ompamba   calabash for drinking

omulongi   teacher

omumwandje   my child

Omuwiliki gwoshituthi   Master of Ceremonies

omuye   wild berry tree

ondjembo yakatusha   Russian rocket launcher

ondjove   marula oil

Ongaame   It is me. (response to a warm welcome)

ontaku   home-made juice, usually a morning drink

ontulo   full flowing dress

ontungwa   large, open basket mainly for carrying food

oompambas   calabashes for drinking; plural of *ompamba*

oontungwas   baskets; plural of *ontungwa*

oonyoka   necklace

opuwo   it's enough

oshigumbo   house of the deceased

oshikumbu   whore, slut

oshikwiila   home-made cake

oshinyanga   a large open hut that is part of the homestead used for meetings; mostly used by men

oshitenga   wooden cup

oshithima   mahangu porridge

Oye naanaa   Here she is. (welcome greeting)

sheeli   short for 'the first-born'

shitenya   daughter-/son-in-law

shiveli   first-born child (affectionate way of addressing a child)

sjali   (Afrikaans) shawl

small mother   aunt

tate   father, sir

te ti   listen

tombo   home-brew

vetkoekies   (Afrikaans) fried fat cakes made of flour

Yakwetu   My goodness.